PARABLES OF HUMAN FRAILTY

DOUGLAS COOP

CONTENTS

To Margaret

PREFACE

Our lives are full of situations that stir our emotions. This has given rise to many parables or morals, each summarising in a few words incidents that are universally true for all time, and could happen to any of us. Each story in *Parables of Human Frailty* begins with a parable that introduces a relevant story. These stories concern very human psychological situations such as the vagaries of love, and illustrate common events. Most of the stories are fiction, but loosely based on actual situations. Several happened to colleagues, while 'The Dreams of Alwyn' and 'The Power of Romance' happened to me years ago.

THE LEGACY

Ridiculing another person may rebound to involve you.

'So you wish to alter your will, doctor?' Young Mr Jones gave a sniff of professional superiority as he thumbed through his legal documents before glancing up at the greying lady seated opposite.

'Yes, Mr Jones,' she replied politely. 'Now I have retired I realise how alone I am in the world. I have nobody to bequeath anything to. As you know I never married, but have devoted a lifetime to caring for my patients.'

'Indeed, doctor, your compassion is a byword in the community,' young Mr Jones replied as he fingered his grey legal tie, a habit of his to draw attention to his status.

'Unfortunately, people soon forget,' she said. 'I'm seldom remembered or recognised in the street now that I have been succeeded by a new doctor with all the latest high-tech equipment.'

'So what would you like me to do, doctor?'

'I have a nest egg of about $50,000, and when I finally depart this life I would like you to arrange a slap-up funeral for me: something for people to talk about.'

'You are not serious,' spluttered young Mr Jones.

'I certainly am! I want to go out with a bang … in a way that I will be remembered.'

'Quite so,' said young Mr Jones wryly.

'I want the cortege to parade through the main street,' she went on enthusiastically. 'And I want the hearse followed by a pipe band playing the "Dead March".'

'Marching girls too?' offered young Mr Jones with a tinge of sarcasm.

'A bit old-fashioned, but what an excellent idea,' she said. 'And I also want you to engage the mayor to deliver an oration at the church, and have a capable journalist supply a glowing eulogy for the press.'

'With all this you will probably get national television coverage,' young Mr Jones added with a snide grin. 'It will cost you a great deal. Just let me give you an estimate. … Ah, yes, you should have some money left over. Let me see … mmm … about $5,000. What would you like to do with that?'

'Ah, that is what I must discuss with you.' She lowered her eyes, and with a faint flush on her cheeks she continued. 'Being unmarried I have often overheard pointed remarks about my private life; people making fun of all I have supposedly missed by remaining single.'

'Go on,' young Mr Jones said, clearing his throat.

'I would like you to arrange for a man to spend the night with me; a man with some experience in that department, to enlighten me with all the alleged pleasures I seem to have neglected. In my day there were far fewer medical women graduates, and most eligible men saw us as too intellectual for them. They called us blue stockings. The only time I was ever with a man was over forty years ago. He was a fellow student with as little experience as me. It was awful, and put me off.'

Young Mr Jones looked at her with barely suppressed amusement. All he saw was a worn-out old lady, thin and bony, and wearing twinset and pearls. Finding a suitable partner for her could be a problem, he concluded.

He could scarcely get home quickly enough to tell his wife about the silly old duck who was prepared to spend $5,000 for her initiation into the joys of marital bliss. He laughed his way through his soup, and was halfway through his steak when his wife fixed him with a determined eye.

'We could do with that money,' she announced in a firm voice. 'It could help pay for your expensive tastes in tailoring.'

The grin melted from his face. 'You're joking …

you're not serious … that bony old woman? … I couldn't …'

'You can, … and I'm serious,' she said. 'The situation requires a youngish man like you with stamina. I'll even drive you to her door and collect you next morning.'

He knew it would be useless to argue with his wife once she had made up her mind, and being a pious man, he took the sensible precaution of crossing himself.

The following Friday evening, after all the arrangements had been made, Mrs Jones packed her husband into their car, and together they drove in silence to the doctor's house; Mrs Jones with a look of resolve and singleness of purpose, her husband resigned and pale, but still hopeful of finding a hole into which he could escape from his distasteful mission. He kept wondering what antics she might want to get up to, and worried about the ignominy of failure. Might it even alter his relationship with his wife? Time for him was rapidly running out, as with an apprehensive step he approached the doctor's ominous door.

Mrs Jones watched her husband in case, at the last minute, his courage should fail him, and saw him pause for some moments before knocking. Seconds later the door opened and he was swallowed into the house. She waited for a few more minutes to ensure he did not try to flee, and then with a shrug of satisfaction drove home with the conviction that the $5,000 was as good as in the bank.

Next morning, sharp at nine-thirty, Mrs Jones drew up again outside the doctor's house and sounded the horn, expecting her husband to burst out of the door and hurry back to her. She anticipated seeing his guilty looks, but she had no intention of embarrassing him by probing for details; after all, it was her idea originally.

The house, however, remained silent, curtains closed and no sign of life. She sounded the horn, and again with no response she marched up the garden path and banged the door knocker. She heard the sound echo inside, but then all remained silent. Perplexed, she returned home wondering.

During the weekend she visited the house again several times without response, finally becoming apprehensive when her husband failed to reappear on two successive evenings.

The following morning she became more persistent with her knocking, and happened to notice a letter-flap near the door. In desperation she pushed it open, and bending down with her mouth at the opening she shouted to her husband. At last a curtain in an upstairs window was drawn aside. His wan face appeared and he called to her.

'Go home, Nora. After our first night together, the doctor has decided to die a pauper!'

2

THE CHINA PARADOX

Never start an affair with no hope of fulfilment.

Perhaps it was the exotic setting of the times that clouded my better judgment, but for the last twenty years the memory has remained fresh in my mind.

I was in Shanghai at the end of a hectic round of business meetings in China, and I had reserved my final day for sightseeing. After making preliminary arrangements with the hotel, the manager met me in the foyer, and I found his charm and politeness typical of the Chinese businessmen I had already had dealings with.

'Come this way, Mr Clark,' he said. 'Our personnel officer is free for the day and has agreed to accompany you to some interesting places.'

With a show of formality he ushered me along the marbled corridors and into a side room where he introduced me to quite the most beautiful Chinese woman I had ever seen. As she rose from behind her desk I suddenly felt so self-conscious in her aura that for several moments I could scarcely look at her.

'This is Sophia, who will escort you,' the manager said. Then noticing my reaction, he added with a smile, 'You will find her eminently suitable for your purpose.' Still smiling, he bowed his way out.

'Have you any plans for today?' Sophia asked in excellent English.

'I'm in your hands,' I stammered, still feeling slightly overwhelmed in her presence. 'But as a memento of my time in Shanghai I would like to photograph some typical Chinese lifestyles.'

'The market would be a good place to start,' she suggested. 'I'll arrange a taxi.'

Once we were seated in the back seat, I quietly turned to look directly towards her; at her exquisite features; at her pale delicate skin, at her brown almond eyes and the sensuous curves of her shape beneath her blue silk dress, split almost to the waist to reveal a long length of thigh, so common in China in those days, so tantalising to me.

After chatting with her for a few minutes I said, 'I find it hard to believe that Sophia is your real name.'

'It's my hotel name,' she replied. 'One we must use with all our guests.'

It was my first experience with a really beautiful woman, but I soon found myself becoming more comfortable in her presence. 'What is your real name?' I asked rather naively. She looked somewhat uneasy at my question, and I noticed a faint blush as she turned her head to look out of the taxi window.

'The hotel does not like us to give our real name to guests.'

I had said the wrong thing and felt rather embarrassed as she continued to gaze out of the window. After several minutes she turned back to me, and with a serene smile on her lips, whispered, 'I am Hu Yan.'

'May I call you Yan? It's such a lovely name.'

For a few seconds Yan continued to smile at me before saying, 'I know your name is Paul. Is it your real name?'

We both smiled at her little joke, and impulsively I reached out and took her hand. She did not withdraw it.

Some minutes later the taxi stopped, and after a few words in Chinese between Yan and the driver, he opened the door for us to step out onto a crowded street. Back home, if a woman with the bearing and beauty of Yan had appeared in public, she would have been met with stares of interest. In Shanghai, nobody but me gave her the slightest attention.

She guided me along a narrow alley that opened at the other end to a large market area: a veritable photographer's dream. There were colourful jugglers, balloon sellers, toy makers, beggars, all actors in a kaleidoscope of activities. Yan led me past a shop selling fish from a pile spilling across the footpath and gutter, while the live fish lay with lethargic movements in tanks of discoloured water. The market was where the average citizen of Shanghai went shopping, and I began to wonder if our hotel purchased its supplies from there.

'Could we move on to see something with more beauty?' I asked Yan.

'There are many beautiful places in Shanghai,' Yan replied as we made our way back to the taxi. 'Allow me to show you.'

Attractive as she was, it was not just her physical grace that impressed me. Rather, it seemed to be some inner charm that enabled her to appreciate and adapt to my wishes without any appearance of compliance. She was able to lead me in a passive way while leaving me with the impression the decisions were all mine. It was an experience quite new to me.

After another taxi ride through crowded streets we stopped beside a long stone wall. Entering under a narrow arched gateway, we found ourselves in the quiet sanctuary of a temple where the fragrant aroma of incense pervaded the air.

'It is necessary for us to remove our shoes,' Yan said as we climbed a flight of stairs and paused outside a dimly lit room.

Inside, and reclining on a couch, was a full-sized Buddha carved from a single block of milk-white jade.

Subdued lighting in an otherwise darkened room gave the Buddha an air of timeless serenity to its pale, almost transparent figure that seemed to radiate a sense of benevolent love.

Alone with Yan in that peaceful tranquillity I glanced at her, and she also seemed quite moved. For some moments we each looked in silence until rashly, I bent and kissed her cheek. She gave a momentary start, and with a look of surprise whispered, 'We must go now.'

We both seemed rather quiet in the taxi until I suggested some afternoon tea. Yan instructed the driver again, and we soon arrived at a new multistorey hotel, all polished marble and expensive Chinese ornamentation. While we were seated in its upmarket restaurant, odd and unsettling doubts began to obtrude about Yan. Who was she really? What was her hotel role? Was she, in fact, just an expensive courtesan working through the hotel? Was I expected to spend the night with her? Anything seemed possible in these exotic surroundings. I recalled the manager's somewhat satisfied smile as he left me alone with Yan that morning. Had he imagined me to be a sophisticated businessman, a man of the world, which I was not? It was time to clear the air.

Seated opposite Yan across a narrow table, I was in a good position to study her expressions and body language.

'Will you be free this evening?' I asked point blank.

'I have to start work at six o'clock,' she answered. 'Normally I start at two o'clock but the manager allowed me the afternoon to assist you.'

'Do you help many guests this way?'

'No, this is the first time.'

I was beginning to feel more relaxed, but decided to probe her further.

'How long have you worked at the hotel?'

'Just three months,' she replied. 'It is only a temporary job for six months to get some experience before returning to university.'

'What do you study there?'

'Engineering. … You look surprised.'

'Frankly, yes,' I said. 'I just can't imagine a beautiful woman with your graceful bearing dressed in overalls and striding about issuing orders on some muddy building site. How did you become interested in such a subject?'

'Both my parents are engineers, and it is only natural that I should follow suit. I have been longing to continue my education in America, but the authorities refused my passport. I will keep trying, but it is so difficult for students to leave China; in the past, so many of them never returned.'

'You will just have to marry a foreigner,' I suggested rather lightly, but immediately regretted having said it. It was an unfortunate remark to make as a joke, but the possibility must have been already taking root in my mind.

'Have you always lived in Shanghai?' I asked, changing the subject.

Yan looked thoughtful for a few moments. 'I was born in the country and came to Shanghai when I was quite young.'

'Born in the country?' I queried after a short silence.

After a further pause she leaned forward and whispered, 'It was a very worrying time for us. We do not like to speak about it. It is all in the past.'

'Was it to do with the Cultural Revolution?' I asked.

After a further pause she regained her composure, adding, 'At that time my parents and their parents were intellectuals living in Shanghai. When my great-uncle was thrown into jail for some supposed crime against the Party, my father used to visit him in the prison to give him a few comforts, or cut his fingernails and beard.'

'That was a brave thing for him to do,' I said.

'It was bad for us, because one rainy night Red Guards banged on my parents' door, and barely gave them time to throw a few clothes into a bag before they hustled them into a van. Some of the guards who spat on my parents were old school friends. Guards drove them to a train full of people in a similar plight, and they were all taken to the country to work in the fields.'

'Do you have any brothers or sisters?' I asked quietly.

'I have one sister, but my parents had to give her away.'

I suddenly remembered that Chinese couples were allowed only one child. 'Do you know where she is?' I asked.

'Oh, yes, we often meet,' she replied. 'We were lucky to have a maiden aunt who was able to take her.' After a further silence Yan suddenly asked, 'How did you have me say so much about myself? All I know about you is that you are a very nice businessman who is treating me with great respect. I really like you. What do you do apart from work?'

'I have little time after work, but at weekends I sometimes play golf.'

'Oh,' she said with a smile. 'That's a game where you hit a ball into a little hole. I once saw it on television.'

'I'm sometimes asked to sing at concerts, too,' I said. 'It's a hobby of mine.'

'How interesting you should do that. In China, musicians have always been rated very low on the social scale, like … mmmm … like street women.'

It was my turn to blush. 'I sing very nice songs, like those from Brahms and Schubert. You may have heard of them.'

'They sound very romantic … and I think you are very romantic, too. I have never heard things like that said here in Shanghai.'

As she gazed at me in what seemed like silent infatuation, I realised I had gone too far for this lovely and gentle girl. Too far for me also, as I began to sense how attracted I was to her. Now, much more at ease with each other, and enjoying our time together, I became aware of a dangerous situation in the making.

'It is almost time for us to return to the hotel,' I said, glancing at my watch with some reluctance.

'I wish we did not have to go,' she said. 'You have given me a most wonderful day, and I do not want you to go away tomorrow.'

We were silent in the taxi, but I noticed a tear well up in Yan's eye and roll down her cheek. Suddenly she turned and gave me a lingering kiss. Our arms went round each other, and we remained in our embrace until nearing the hotel.

'Write to me, and I will keep trying for a passport.' A woman's whisper can be more compelling than a spoken request. In a moment she was gone, leaving my cheeks wet with her tears.

I remained restless all evening, resisting the temptation of visiting her at work, as it would surely embarrass her in front of others. But I did leave her a heart-shaped box of chocolates carefully gift-wrapped in paper inscribed with words I had dared not say aloud to her.

Next morning at the airport, and after an uneasy night, I was waiting dejectedly for my flight to Hong Kong, when I caught a glimpse of Yan hurrying towards me in the crowds. In moments she was in my arms.

'I've never been so glad to see anyone,' I said.

'I was afraid I had arrived too late,' she said. 'I tried so hard to stay away, but couldn't without seeing you just once more. This is a brief moment of double happiness for us. Please write to me, and I will keep trying for a passport.'

The call to board the aircraft came all too soon. As I turned to give a final wave, I could see Yan standing there, looking so beautiful, so vulnerable, so despondent. I don't remember much of that flight; just sitting there dejected; reliving each single minute of the previous day with Yan; wondering what to do about it.

Back home I remained in a quandary, my mind in turmoil. Perhaps her love for me would fade as rapidly as it flared. On the other hand, it would be heartless of me to begin a romantic correspondence with her if she could never leave China. Then again, I could return to China and marry her. As my wife, she would surely be able to leave. But would she be able to adapt to a foreign country? She could become very lonely away from all her relatives and friends. That would not be in her best interests.

I never wrote to her. I didn't know what to do about it.

Two years later I received a letter from Yan, written from America. It contained an invitation to her wedding in New York. She was to marry a Chinese university professor. Clearly she had attained her wish of getting to America. But why send me an invitation to her wedding? Perhaps her love for me was genuine, and she wanted to see me once again, and for the last time.

I did not go to the wedding, but sent a handmade glass jug, red for good fortune. I never heard from Yan again, but I hope her new life in America is bringing her the happiness she deserves.

3

SNAKES ALIVE

Prudent people will prepare for the unexpected.

Throughout summer the torrid sun bore down relentlessly on the small outback Australian town, leaving its sweltering residents listless and languid. In the parched countryside the river had become reduced to a series of waterholes, and in the scintillating atmosphere an occasional willy-willy would swirl dust into a miniature whirlpool before settling again. There seemed to be no escape from the oppressive heat haze that sucked out vitality.

'Much more of this and we will both look like dried-out corks,' said Dr Williams as he poured himself another whisky and soda before settling back again under a ceiling fan to read his medical journal.

'Oh Basil, it's the poor farmers I'm sorry for,' said his wife from the kitchen. 'At least they have the decency not to bother you in all this heat, and there are only two patients in the hospital.'

'Yes, I'll probably discharge old Harry tomorrow. He has finally dried out, and stopped seeing snakes everywhere. Now I have his diabetes under control, his problems will be solved; that is if he can stay sober. It just leaves Mrs McPherson. Now her heart is better behaved, I'm thinking of taking out her drip tomorrow, and her other tubes later on.'

'Poor Mrs McPherson, nothing seems to go right for her these days,' his wife said, as she came through to join her husband. 'With her son going away and leaving her and her old husband to manage the property, it's no wonder she had a heart attack.'

'Well, Betty, despite those first few worrying days, she is much happier than being sent away to a base hospital,' Dr Williams replied.

His wife nodded. 'In the months we have been here,' she said, 'you have earned the confidence of the whole region.'

'Well, after growing up in a big city, I like the challenge of this isolated area. Anyway, Betty, once we can afford it, we should buy into a city practice. Life would be less of a struggle as we get older, and the children's education—'

His conversation was suddenly cut short by a ring on his cellphone.

'Oh doctor, can you come to the hospital quickly.' The matron's voice conveyed a sense of urgency. 'It's

Mrs McPherson ... she has just rushed into my office with all her tubes dangling from her ... said she saw a snake in her room.'

'Good Lord,' said the doctor. 'She must be hallucinating. Give her a nip of brandy and I'll be right over.'

On his way to the hospital he pondered why she should imagine she was seeing snakes. The drugs she is on are an unlikely cause, he thought. Then again, perhaps she is a secret drinker. There are several outback women I know who comfort their loneliness and boredom in this way, and Mrs McPherson has been in hospital long enough for the DTs to catch up. By the time he reached the hospital he had her firmly diagnosed as a chronic alcoholic, and with a confident step he strode along the corridor and into the matron's office.

'So there you are, Mrs McPherson. What is this I hear about you seeing snakes?'

'Just one snake, doctor.' By this time she had regained her composure, but still looked rather pitiful sitting there with all the tubes and wires dangling from her.

'Just one ...?' he queried with some surprise. 'Are you sure?'

'Yes, doctor, I was simply lying there in bed trying to keep cool when something caught my attention out of the corner of my eye. There to my horror I saw a large black snake almost a couple of metres long coming through the doorway, and heading towards my bed. I gave a scream, and without thinking sprang out of bed and ran to the matron's office.'

'Are you sure you were not dreaming?' asked the doctor, hopefully.

'No, doctor, I've seen enough of them to know a black snake when I see one, and this one was very real.'

'Well, you'll just have to catch it, won't you, doctor?' said the matron with a certain challenge in her voice.

It was the first live snake the city-bred doctor had ever had to deal with, and he hoped neither of the two women noticed his sudden pallor. Drawing himself up to his full height, he said, 'Get me a broom, matron, one with a heavy end. Now both you ladies stay here.'

He took the broom, and waggling it like a golf club, managed to muster a sickly smile for the two women. As he left the office he thought he heard Mrs McPherson say, 'Isn't he wonderful!', quite unaware of how much he was shaking inwardly.

He made his cautious way to the women's end of the hospital, glancing into various rooms until he came to the one Mrs McPherson had fled from. Approaching the door with some trepidation, he peered in with his broom at the ready. There, ensconced on the bed, was a large black snake. When it saw Dr Williams, it made a lightning movement onto the floor and came straight towards him. But on the highly polished floor it was at a distinct disadvantage. Despite its frantic efforts to escape, its progress became very sluggish, making it an easy target for Dr Williams' broom head.

'It is quite safe for you to come back to your room now, Mrs McPherson,' said Dr Williams with some relief, but without confessing the snake had been so hindered by the highly polished floor. 'It must have come into the hospital to get out of the heat, and lost its way.'

'If there was one snake in the hospital, there may be others about,' said Mrs McPherson, as she was being reattached to her tubes.

'I take your point,' said Dr Williams. 'I'll arrange for an official catcher to come as soon as possible to check everywhere.'

Two mornings later a snake catcher flew in by light plane and soon began a preliminary inspection of the hospital and its grounds. He was a large moon-faced man of middle age and jovial manners. Despite the late-morning heat, he busied himself poking about under bushes and ornamental shrubs.

'You should keep your grass shorter,' he advised before scrambling under the hospital.

To pass the time of day the pilot, who had little else to do, strolled across to the matron's office to relax under her ceiling fan and drink iced coffee. Their conversation soon turned to snakes. 'Better him than me,' the pilot confessed. 'He seems to enjoy his work, but I feel safer flying.'

In the early afternoon the doctor returned and joined the snake catcher. 'Any developments?' he asked.

'The grounds are clear,' the catcher replied. 'But I'm about to go back under the hospital again. There's a pile of old wood under there, probably left when the hospital was altered several years ago. If there are any snakes about, that is where they will be living.'

Seeing them talking together, the pilot sauntered across to join the conversation.

'I'm going under again,' said the catcher. 'Will you hold the bag open, doc, in case I catch something?'

'Well … I'm a bit short of time … actually,' said the doctor. 'Can you leave the bag with your pilot?'

'Hang on, mate,' said the catcher. 'I don't want anything to happen to him. I need him to fly me out of here this afternoon.'

But Dr Williams had become so self-absorbed by the comment that he did not notice the catcher's broad wink.

'Just hold the top of the bag open, doc, and I'll drop the snake in. Don't be slow in shutting it.' With that the catcher disappeared under the hospital.

'You have to hand it to him,' the pilot said as they both began to feel somewhat anxious.

'Get ready, doc,' came the catcher's voice. 'Here's our first.' Moments later he emerged with a tiger snake drooping over the crook of his catching pole. He dropped the snake tail first into the open sack held by the doctor, who wasted no time in twisting it shut. The catcher quickly vanished under the hospital again.

Suddenly, there was a shout and a curse from under the hospital and the catcher reappeared.

'Have you been bitten?' shouted the doctor.

'Bloody hell, no,' replied the catcher, 'but if I have to find more snakes I'll have to clear out all this mess of timber down there. Curse those lazy builders.'

The catcher soon had a stack of timber ends piled on the lawn, and he reappeared once more. 'There are snakes in all directions down there,' he shouted, and turning to the pilot he said, 'Run and organise a torch for me. It's pretty dark in some of the corners.'

'Snakes in all directions,' mused the doctor. 'I hope he is exaggerating.'

As the afternoon progressed, the catcher emerged from time to time with more snakes, which he dropped carefully into sacks that the doctor held open. He caught five in all until he was satisfied none was left.

'Time for cold drinks,' called the matron, who had come across to check on progress. 'Come inside out of all this heat.'

When they were seated in her office, tensions were released in laughter.

'I hope you have tied the sacks securely, doc,' said the catcher. 'Snakes have been known to escape,' and with a broad wink added, 'I would hate to see Nobby here trying to fly me home with a cabin full of angry tiger snakes.' It was the pilot's turn to blanch.

'How can we be certain the hospital will be safe in the future?' asked the matron next day.

'Oh, just make sure you keep all the floors well polished,' Dr Williams answered casually.

She gave him a quizzical look.

4

HENRIETTA

*In the right circumstances, old love may be triggered to
resurface.*

After driving all through the day, Harry became
aware of an almost overpowering sense of
fatigue. It annoyed him to remember how once he
could have driven the whole journey and still felt fresh.
Now at fifty-five he realised his stamina was failing,
and Wellington was still over an hour away. Speeding
on in the setting sun, he began to feel mesmerised by
long scintillating shadows across the tree-lined road,
until his growing sense of drowsiness ended with a
sudden involuntary jerk, making him aware of drifting
into momentary sleep.

I had better slow down and stop at the next motel,
he thought, and to avoid any further loss of concentration he wound down his window to gasp in large gulps

of air. By now the late-afternoon traffic was beginning to build up, giving him concern that his slower speed might tempt following cars to pass dangerously. At the same time, he became uneasy with the thought that any further lapse of concentration might lead to his drifting into oncoming traffic. It was another ten minutes before he was relieved to see a large roadside sign pointing towards a country motel.

Turning into its long gravel driveway, he could see a group of white stucco buildings scattered randomly across well-mown lawns, and in the distance, a calm sea lapping gently onto the grey sand of a small curved beach.

He continued along an access road lined with flowering camellias, and with the sounds of loose shingle crepitating under his tyres he reached the parking area. He continued to sit there for a few moments before gathering energy to step out and stretch his limbs. A cool breeze refreshed him, but he knew it would be foolish to continue driving.

Finding the office deserted, he rang the bell, and leaning against the counter began to browse through a few brochures on a nearby table. He soon heard the approach of footsteps, and a shapely woman entered, her friendly smile freezing to a pallid stare when she saw him.

'Harry Smith,' she burst out in surprise. Then, in a voice that sank to a whisper, 'You are the last person I would ever wish to see again.'

For a moment Harry was taken aback. 'Why, Ruth. It's you … what a coincidence after all these years.'

She continued to stare indignantly before asking, 'Under the circumstances, do you really need to stay here?'

'If you have a room,' he answered defensively. 'I haven't the strength to keep driving. I'm staggered to find you so bitter towards me, but I can understand.'

'Room seven,' she said in a cold tone, and handed him the keys.

'Ruth, believe me, I had no option all those years ago.'

'No option? … You promised to marry me, and I let you … well, never mind. Then, within a month you broke it off without an explanation, and in no time had married Anne. What was I to think of you?'

'I was trapped, Ruth. Anne's parents were old family friends, and just before you and I became engaged they invited me to Anne's twenty-first birthday party. All I remember is there was a lot of drinking.'

Ruth looked at him with undisguised contempt, and half-turning away, added with strained courtesy, 'Your room is to the right as you leave.'

Harry hesitated for a few moments, and regaining a little confidence, knew it would be his only opportunity for an explanation. Gathering his resolve he went on to say, 'Soon after you and I became engaged, to my dismay, Anne came to me saying she was pregnant. She told me it must have happened at the party, not that I have any memory of the event, but a great deal of family pressure was put on me to marry her.'

'You might have told me about it at the time,' Ruth replied with some disgust.

'I was young then, and too distressed to think straight. I imagined a quick severance would be best for both of us.'

Ruth's quizzical look suggested to him that he should have been more forthright at the time.

'Anyway,' he continued hopefully, 'a couple of months after we married, Anne had a miscarriage and I was left with a wife I had not bargained for, while you had gone out of my life.'

Ruth gave a short sigh. Was it sympathy, or impatience, he wondered? He could not tell, but it gave him the courage to continue. 'Anne and I stayed together and raised a family, but she developed a long-standing illness and passed away last year. However, enough of that. Tell me about yourself, Ruth.'

'There is nothing much to say, except I am looking after the motel while my daughter and her husband, who own it, are taking a well-deserved break.'

As she continued to talk about her daughter, Harry had the impression she was becoming more affable. Instinctively, he began to appraise her in a more masculine way. This was the woman he had once loved with a romantic passion that had filled his days with new enchantment. After his untimely marriage to Anne he had often felt somehow cheated, but accepted a situation that was of his own making.

With the passing years, his love for Ruth had become submerged in the hurly-burly of career and family life, and he had to admit he had almost forgotten her.

As they began to chat more freely, her tense expression began to relax, and Harry soon noticed the suggestion of a smile would flit across her face. Now feeling more comfortable in her company, he said, 'I am feeling weary. I would appreciate your showing me to my room.'

Strolling the short distance together in the twilight seemed to draw Harry closer. From somewhere deep inside him details of half-forgotten memories returned like an apparition to stir his old yearning for Ruth. He saw in her the indefinable beauty, which he imagined came from her enthusiasm and satisfaction of a successful life. Or could it be, he wondered, a secret pleasure in seeing him again?

While they sat chatting in his room, a sudden feeling of jealousy came into Harry's mind, as he thought of her being married to someone who could share with her all the pleasures he had once dreamed of for himself. He remembered his own marriage, empty by comparison, and atrophied through years of uneventful living.

At that moment there came a knock at the door. Ruth opened it to reveal a young woman who said, 'I noticed these lights on. We are home again; we'll see you in the morning.'

After the exchange of a few more words, Ruth closed the door and looked at Harry. 'My daughter and her husband are back, and will be having an early night after their travels.'

But Harry remained uneasy. The woman at the door reminded him of his mother. She had the same unusual dark blue eyes and fair hair. It could have been my mother standing there, he thought. A creepy feeling came over him as he realised she might even be his daughter. But that did not make sense to him.

With some embarrassment he averted his eyes and in a quiet voice asked, 'Is your husband with you?'

For a moment Ruth was silent before giving an instinctive toss of her head. 'I never married,' she said.

'But Ruth ...' he stammered. 'Your daughter?'

'She is our daughter, Harry,' Ruth replied. As she spoke, she became aware of a warmth creeping into her cheeks, and realised she must be blushing

Harry's mouth half opened, and she heard his sudden intake of breath. The charm that he had seen in her now turned to alarm at any implications this might have for him.

'You should have told me at the time,' he stammered, not knowing how he would have reacted had she done so.

'I didn't know I was pregnant when you walked out on me,' she said. 'With nobody to turn to I left town in shame. It was my first step into a long loneliness that was helped only after the arrival of Henrietta. I named her after you, Harry, and raised her on my own, and we have always been very close.'

Harry continued to regard her in silence, not knowing how to respond, but it seemed to him that she was relieved to be telling him about her difficult past. At least she appeared to be more affable towards him. He concluded she must still carry some spark of attraction towards him. He decided her earlier rejection of him had simply concealed a desire to keep old wounds closed.

Perhaps I should have driven away with her first hint, he thought. But now with an uneasy conscience he felt compassion for her, and in his remorse wondered if in any way he could make amends.

'Ruth,' he began shakily, 'I'm quite dismayed by these revelations, but glad of this chance meeting. I have a great deal to make up to you. Could we perhaps become friends again?'

'It was the early years that were so difficult for me,' she replied, avoiding the question. 'But now I have had the joy of rearing Henrietta, and know she is happily married, I would not want to change anything ... but yes ... I suppose we could be friends, at least for our daughter's sake.'

Harry's face brightened. Seeing Ruth again he could detect a spark of the old attraction to each other, but knew it would take time to heal the deep rift between them. He reached out and gently took her hand with hopes that their new friendship might in time develop into something deeper.

'You must be starving,' Ruth said lightly. 'I'll get you a meal, and afterwards I'll show you my photographs of Henrietta. Tomorrow you could meet her in person.'

Harry took a step closer and gently kissed Ruth on the cheek.

5

EPILOGUE TO TEMPTATION

Rumour is prone to lead to drama and overreaction.

Giving a guilty start, I slowly dropped the newspaper to my knees, as half-suppressed memories began to surge back to me.

'What is it, Frank?' From across the hotel room my wife's voice jolted me out of my thoughts.

'Oh, it's nothing,' I replied as casually as possible. 'It's just the death notice of my old landlady from my student days here in Dunedin. After all these years it's quite a fluke that we should be passing through the old town at this time.'

Picking up the paper again, mainly to hide any signs of embarrassment, I found my thoughts returning to a time over twenty years previously when I had first come to Dunedin as a young university student. Tall and athletic, I had arrived full of ambition to succeed.

After the first year I had outgrown my residential college and the other young students who lived there. To gain independence I took lodgings for the next two years in a rather run-down boarding house near the university. The landlady, a motherly old thing, as I thought, gave me my meals on time and did my washing.

I remember how she showed me into my small room that was to be my home for the next two years. I became used to the drab, worn carpet, the narrow bed, and the desk by the window where each day I could look out to a tiny garden, and watch the changing seasons. On a clear night I could even see the stars.

After about six months an out-of-town uncle, a worldly and forthright man, paid me a brief visit, and stayed for supper. As he was about to leave he hesitated for a moment as if in thought before asking, 'Do you realise your landlady is in love with you?'

'You are having me on,' I burst out in surprise.

'No, Frank,' he said. 'I've been watching her during supper, and there is no doubt about it.'

'But she is over twice my age; she's well into her forties.'

'Love is no respecter of age, Frank. It can happen to anyone quite unexpectedly.'

I was left pondering the implications, but finally dismissed the idea as too bizarre. Even so, it is strange how a simple remark, casually made, can sometimes change a person's life.

Soon my curiosity became aroused, and I began to pay more attention to her; watching unobserved, seeking some token of affection, but all I saw was a lonely woman with sagging breasts and work-worn hands. Fine lines engraved on her face and about her eyes showed that her youthful femininity had long-since dried. She appeared to be a woman cheated by time and misfortune. I wondered what my uncle had really noticed.

Despite my doubts, I soon began to sense a growing temptation wakening in my young mind, goading me between desire and what I felt might be achieved. I decided to become more daring and put her to the test, reasoning I had little to lose. After all, student life requires more than just studying.

The following evening, when she brought my supper, I reached out, and clasping her hands, began to gaze intently at her palms.

'What are you looking at?' she asked.

'I'm reading your fortune,' I answered confidently, despite my meagre knowledge of palmistry.

Over the next few evenings this apparent interest in her as a person gave her the confidence to unleash a torrent of emotions. She poured out the heartache of her childless marriage. How others in the family all had children to love and care for, but they never visited her. She relived the death of her husband, and told how she had nursed him through a long-standing illness, and hinted that her lonely life was the reason for taking me as her first boarder. Listening sympathetically to all she had to say, I encouraged her with murmurs of interest, even offering her a handkerchief when tears seemed imminent.

Later in the week, as she cleared the evening dishes, I summoned the gall to clasp her shoulders and, bending down, my lips touched her cheek with a lingering kiss. After a moment she stepped back with a look of startled surprise.

'You shouldn't do that,' she whispered, but as she left the room I detected her rather subtle smile. For a few moments I stood wondering what secret desires might lie behind her dull eyes. That evening, as I studied, I could hear the sounds of humming from the kitchen. I hoped it was an indication of the womanhood I had roused in her.

After returning from lectures the next afternoon, I found her smiling and friendly with much to tell me of her day at home. Boring as it was, I let her prattle on through the evening meal, even helping her to wash the dishes. It was during that time I saw her in a new light. She seemed to have become much younger, with movements of natural grace, and for the first time I heard her laugh. A suggestion of coyness in her conversation left me wondering how long she could stand against this ruthless current of temptation.

As we chatted pleasantly together, passion began to cloud my reason, and in the heat of desire I took her in my arms. She looked up at me bewildered as I bent, giving her an impassioned kiss on her mouth. For several moments she fused into my embrace, our bodies moulding against each other as our lips moved sensually together.

Trembling, she broke from my grasp, whispering, 'You are a naughty boy.'

The lack of conviction in her voice encouraged me to say, 'Since living here I'm away all day and come home at night to study, knowing you are here to care for me. It's almost like being married.'

'What are you suggesting?' she murmured in an innocent tone of voice.

'We are both lonely people,' I said. 'Let us start living as a couple.'

'You are very persuasive,' she said, in a voice betraying passionate agreement. Moments later we were again enfolded in a mutual embrace.

As I led her to my bedroom I could feel the pounding of her heart beneath my hand. Words had now become inappropriate as I began to gently remove her worn jersey and dress. I had never before had the opportunity of coping with a mature woman with her defences down. Putting doubts aside I proceeded slowly and carefully to remove further layers of her clothing, prepared to stop at any sign of resistance. I told myself that in the past she must have been a full-blooded woman with her feminine urges met by a devoted husband. Now, after years of loneliness, she must surely yield to this unexpected bonus.

I found her body soft and warm, with breasts fuller than they had appeared beneath her loose dress. All the time I felt acutely aware of her rapid breathing and pulse, hoping neither would wane. It was she who removed my clothing, and for the first time, each saw the other naked. Lying, limbs folded around each other, our bodies throbbed with an intensity that left us relaxed in each other's arms.

The next day I could scarcely concentrate on my lectures, my thoughts constantly returning to the ecstasies of the previous night. Flushed with the success of the escapade, I was only vaguely aware that this hopeful quest for ephemeral pleasures would lead to a hell of my own making. As desire overcame discretion, I gave little thought to my landlady's feelings. As a callow youth I saw her only as an unfulfilled woman grasping at this unexpected opportunity. I was too young to realise my conduct had transferred her feelings of affection into deep, passionate love. I simply imagined her emotions were as shallow as mine, and in the end both of us would escape any consequences.

In her newfound confidence she began to dress elegantly. With well-chosen clothes and foundation garments together with a modern hairstyle, she had become transformed into an attractive and charming middle-aged woman. I learned her name was Pauline, a name I thought fitted her new personality well.

At first I thought myself fortunate to have found this ready-made outlet for my youthful ardour without anyone suspecting. But as the weeks passed I slowly became aware of a negative side. Instead of coming home, as formerly, to a quiet evening of study, I found myself becoming disorganised by a seductive woman with all day to dream of nightly pleasures in store. As she continued to demand more of my time, my studies became further disrupted until it became obvious to me I had fallen into my own trap.

Finally, I insisted on having the evenings to myself for study if I was going to pass my exams. Although she agreed reluctantly, I could tell her eyes still signalled the same old crackle of fire. And on returning to my books I seemed to lack my former concentration. When I returned home for the long summer vacation I just moped about the house, unable to interest myself in anything. When the holiday came to a close I could hardly wait to get back to Dunedin. Pauline greeted me with genuine affection, and almost immediately we were in each other's arms again, rejoicing in the joy of reunion.

During the year we managed to act with enough decorum for me to cope with my course of lectures. Like any married couple we shared a bed at night, but went our separate ways during the day. We never attended any function together, or went anywhere where we might be recognised. I'm sure I could never have weathered the good-natured banter of my friends if they had caught me in the company of a middle-aged woman. They would have been genuinely sorry for me if they knew Pauline was my landlady. Had they only known. At the end of the year I did not go to any of the student celebrations, but stayed with Pauline and waited until the moment seemed right to broach the subject and have a final discussion with her.

'Now, with studies finished,' I began rather formally, 'it's getting time for me to move north to start my new job.' As I spoke, her face took on the pallor of one condemned, and she sat with downcast eyes, looking so forlorn and vulnerable. At first she made no attempt to speak while her body shook with barely suppressed anguish. Then, as if voicing an unwanted decision, she looked up to me, saying, 'I have held you back for long enough … we must part for ever.'

I had not expected Pauline to be so candid and straight to the point. 'Couldn't we meet again sometimes in the future?' I asked hopefully.

'Life is full of desires we can never bring about,' she said quietly. As I stammered a reply, she added a final blow to me. 'If I made any attempt to continue our association, you would come to hate me. You have brought me more pleasure and fulfilment to my life than I have ever known. Let us remember our love in this way.'

As year followed year, memories of her and our secret passion slowly faded from my thoughts … until now.

'Will you be going to the funeral?' my wife asked.

'I suppose I should go,' I answered, trying to appear nonchalant.

The funeral was a sad affair; only a few people attended, and after the service one man approached me.

'Did you know my sister?' he asked.

'She was my landlady years ago.'

'Poor girl,' he said. 'She was always rather frail, and had an unfortunate life, but she worked hard when she was able.'

'She seemed fine when I knew her in my student days. She was kind and thoughtful, and looked after me well.'

'You must have been an early student,' he said. 'After the first one or two she developed a long-standing depression that did not fully respond to treatment. The doctor thought she was troubled by some long-standing sadness; probably a result of the loss of her husband.'

'Yes,' I mused, as a deep feeling of guilt welled up in me. 'Yes, that must surely have been the reason.'

SECRET ENCOUNTER

Some people will go to great lengths to attain their desires.

The morning dawned just as hot and sticky as I had expected it would be in Manila. As I emerged from the air conditioning of the international hotel, other guests had already begun to congregate around the swimming pool set in exotic gardens under perfumed and flowering trees. Snatches of conversation from the many nationalities gathering there drifted across the still air to give an abstract sense of time and space. Only thirty-six hours before, I had been working on a bleak and windy day in Wellington. Now, having changed my grey professional suit for the casual clothes of a tourist, I was ready to enjoy the informality of a tropical holiday.

Surrounded by this exotic luxury, I strolled across to

the activity around the pool, and sat at the only vacant table to enjoy my ice-cool orange drink and watch the other guests lazing in the water. As I sat there, lethargic in the sultry air, and thinking about nothing in particular, my peace of mind was suddenly shattered by a woman who came into view and sat down opposite me at the table. Conversation was the last thing on my mind, and I completely ignored her, apart from noticing she was probably in her mid-thirties, and from the numerous rings on her fingers, I took her for an American. I could see from her downcast eyes and wistful expression that her thoughts lay elsewhere.

Then for the second time that morning my tranquillity was broken, this time by the harsh sounds of a voice from just behind me.

'So there you are!' it boomed. 'Still sulking, I see.'

Coming around the table, a large man with a bull neck and red face sat down, glaring at the woman.

'I would have left you back home if I had thought you were going to be so childish. Well, I'm leaving you behind today to finish your sulking while the rest of us go sightseeing.'

As he continued to upbraid her, I remained expressionless. I took no notice of either of them, but kept watching the people in the pool, as if I was one of the international set that did not speak English. Finally, he strode off looking rather ridiculous in a pair of baggy floral shorts that reached below his knees.

His wife continued to sit silently for some

moments, as if uncertain what to do. Then gathering her bag, she was about to rise when I looked at her across the table.

'I'm appalled to hear someone rebuke his wife like that in public,' I heard myself say.

She gave me a startled look. Then without a word she began to rise. She was almost upright when she paused, as if in a quandary, and she sat down again. We looked at one another in silence, as if not knowing what to say. She was quite tall and shapely, and I wondered what cause she could have given her husband to treat her so rudely. Finally, I broke the silence.

'Your husband seems very uptight this morning. I couldn't help overhearing him, and apologise if my presence has caused you any embarrassment.'

'It is Jed who has caused my embarrassment, not you,' she replied.

Once the ice was broken we chatted pleasantly together for some time before I suggested rather hopefully, 'With Jed away for the day, why not spend the day together? It could do us both good.'

After a long pause, as if coming to a decision, she gave me an amused smile as she said, 'Why not? I'll meet you here in half an hour.'

In her absence I sat contemplating this unexpected turn of events, with its prospect of attractive company, and promise of a few hours of life's ephemeral pleasures.

On her return she seemed more composed, and I was surprised to find her a sophisticated woman; quite the opposite of my earlier impression. We could not have found a more romantic setting than in the perfumed flower gardens of the hotel to be together. Later, while strolling under the shade of the trees I sensed a ring of enchantment to my thoughts, and sought to find any suggestion of secret desires behind her smiling eyes. However, she did not flirt or give any other subtle hints. Her conversation remained friendly and entertaining, as if we had known each other for years.

I remained guessing why she had decided to spend her day with me, a complete stranger. At the same time she seemed the wrong person to be married to someone like her husband. Perhaps in his absence she was just filling in what would otherwise be a boring day; or was it the womanhood in her seeking more?

At last the moment seemed right for me to drop my first tongue-in-cheek hint. 'We are getting along so well, other guests will naturally assume we are long-since married.'

'I'm certainly happier than I was this morning with Jed,' she admitted. 'He is very frustrated at present.'

'Very frustrated?' I prompted.

'He has always hoped, without success, for a son to succeed him in business.'

'Does he blame you for this?' I asked.

'He did for a long time, but finally, tests showed the fault to be his.'

'He seems to be taking it badly.'

'As you saw, he is a macho man, and it took him a long time to come to terms with his problem. He hasn't given up hope that he could come right on this holiday; but I doubt it. If we have no luck, we have agreed to accept a donor when we get back.'

But, already an obvious scheme was forming in my mind, although I sensed it was too soon to suggest it. I had the feeling she was deliberately preparing the ground for me; playing hard to get, taking time to sound me out before making a final commitment, but leaving me with the feeling it was me making the decisions; very clever of her.

After a satisfying lunch and a glass of Pinot Noir, we both continued to find much in common. It was then I broached my ultimate intention.

'Would you care to come up to my room for a cup of coffee?' I suggested.

She gave me a knowing look, and with a smile she said, 'I'm really not that sort of person.'

'It's not just for us,' I replied, having laid my cards on the table. 'It's for you and Jed. Think how delighted he would be not to have the ignominy of a donor back home.'

'I'll have to think it over,' she answered with a slight smile.

I took her remark to mean she still had a little mock

resistance for me to overcome. As we continued talking I began to notice a subtle change in her, an almost coquettishness in her demeanour. Her features took on a more alluring expression, and she giggled once or twice. I knew then that she had made up her mind. Strolling through the hotel's perfumed gardens she grasped my bare arm, and with our fingers entwined like first love, she conversed in tones of suppressed excitement. As we walked along the path, our hips together, I could feel her thigh pressing against mine with every step. We entered the hotel separately, rejoining in the lift.

'We will have to do this properly,' I said, as I closed the bedroom door behind us.

'Of course,' she whispered, in a tone of yielding tenderness.

Moving up behind her, I put both my arms around her waist, and resting my chin on her shoulder, began to caress her hair with my cheek. After a few moments she turned to face me, and it was then we kissed for the first time. As she clung to me in a submissive embrace, I could feel the pounding of her heart against me.

Drawing the curtains to admit only a faint light, I took her in my arms again and held her closely to me. I could guess her emotions were running high, since after all, she was the one who was to receive the gift of a new life from me; someone for her to love and cherish always. I just happened to be her transient accomplice.

Never before had I experienced the sensuous passions of that afternoon, or the profound mental satisfaction in giving her a new life. There could be no doubt in either of our minds that something momentous had happened between us.

We continued to caress and kiss throughout the afternoon until she sat up, saying, 'Jed will soon be back. I must go.'

The world of reality had returned for me. As we lingered over a cup of coffee, I said, 'Strange how we know each other so intimately, but I do not know your married name.'

'It's best you do not know,' she replied. 'At some future date you may want to search out your child. That could cause untold problems for all concerned.'

I could see her point of view, and as I opened the door for us to leave she turned, giving me a glance of passionate understanding. 'Don't come with me; some of Jed's group may have returned.'

I watched her walk down the corridor; her body filled with new allure gave a lightness to her step. At the lift she turned and waved. That was our last direct communication.

As I closed the door I began to wonder if it had all been an illusion, but the sight of two empty coffee cups on the table brought me back to reality. My mind began to crowd with doubts. What if Jed suspected something? What would he do? What if he wanted a DNA test? What would become of her and our child? He seemed the sort who could cause trouble.

That evening in the hotel restaurant she and Jed took a table near me, where I could hear the boom of his voice above the music. He seemed to be outlining his day of sightseeing, and no doubt telling her of all she had missed. I caught her eye once or twice, but she rightly gave no sign of recognition. I did, however, suspect a look of secret happiness behind her bland expression.

I never saw her again, but somehow she must have obtained my email address, because almost a year later I received a brief note from her.

'Our son born a month ago. Jed ecstatic. Love, Carol.

7

THE STALKER

Stalking the doctor is one of the hazards of medical practice.

D r White had no sooner arrived home at the end of a long day, when his cellphone rang. As this was a common event in his life, he had become accustomed to interruptions at mealtime by patients seeking free advice. Also, being the police doctor he was used to calls any time of the day or night to examine drunken drivers or suicides.

He handed the phone to his wife to answer, as she protected him in this way, and he sauntered through to the lounge to sit on a comfortable chair. He could hear the distant sounds of her conversation, and in a few minutes she came into the room with a broad smile.

'You will have to sort this out for yourself,' she said. 'Some woman wants to talk to you about a personal problem. It's something to do with sexual harassment at work.'

'Oh, not another one,' he sighed, as he took the phone from his wife.

'Yes, how can I help you?' he asked in his usual professional manner.

'Thank you, doctor, for talking with me,' exclaimed a rather agitated woman's voice. 'I have rung you because I have nobody else to turn to for advice.'

'Yes,' replied Dr White. 'Please go on.'

'I work in a government department, but in recent months my supervisor has harassed me so often that it has affected my work. Everybody is beginning to think I am inefficient. But it is just that I can't concentrate.'

'What form does this harassment take?' asked Dr White.

'It all began when a new supervisor took over the office,' the voice said. 'He seemed to notice me, and it wasn't long before he would draw up a chair beside my computer, allegedly to help.'

'What would happen then?' he asked.

'He would keep rubbing his leg against mine, or he would reach across in front of me, and just happen to brush across my breast.'

'Did you ever object?'

'I didn't like to say anything to him because he was my boss, and middle-aged at that. It was very embarrassing.'

Dr White heard her voice become more agitated as

she added, 'It all came to a head several weeks ago when he suggested we spend a night together.'

'How did you take that?' Dr White asked.

'I told him I was insulted. He then said I would be sorry I had been so uncooperative.'

After a pause to regain her composure, she continued. 'He seldom spoke to me again, but several days ago I received a notice to appear before a disciplinary committee for a review of a bad work report.'

'No doubt his attempt to ease you out of his department,' concluded the doctor.

'Yes,' said the woman. 'Such a black mark could affect my whole career in the public service. I have rung you in desperation, hoping you could advise me how I should deal with it.'

Dr White was thoughtful for a few moments before replying. 'You should have been firm with him from the start. When he continued to bother you, you should have asked a male friend to ring the supervisor's wife to tell her he was sexually harassing his female staff. She would tell him a thing or two! It may not be the first time he has tried it on. He would conclude his wife's phone call came from one of his office colleagues who had seen him in action.'

'I'm afraid it is too late for that now,' the woman sighed.

After another brief pause Dr White resumed. 'You should be honest with this committee. Tell them what you have told me. Be sure to get one or two people, preferably previous supervisors, to testify your previous work was satisfactory.'

'Thank you so much for your advice,' she said. 'I have been so devastated in the last few days that I haven't been able to think straight.'

Dr White promptly put the incident out of his mind, and settled back to watch the evening news.

About three weeks later he had a further ring from the woman. She told him in an excited voice that she had taken his advice. Gathering her breath, she said that the committee had not only recommended a transfer for the supervisor, but had given her a promotion. 'I am ever so thankful for what you have done to help me,' she said.

The next day he saw her for the first time. She arrived at his surgery carrying a parcel wrapped in fancy paper. She flounced into his surgery displaying a ready friendliness that belied an underlying nervousness at this, their first meeting. With a gesture, Dr White indicated a chair, which for the moment she ignored, greeting him with a hand outstretched for him to shake, and introducing herself as Sonja Smith.

He had expected a shy, mousy person; probably someone easily led. He now found himself confronted by an attractive and charismatic woman. For a few seconds he was nonplussed, but during that brief period he became aware of her pretty face and fair complexion, with a mass of blonde curls falling down over her neck. As she sat, crossing her legs, the hem of her silk frock slipped up to reveal the unexpected bonus of shapely thighs.

This woman is naive and has a frail personality, he thought as he accepted her gift. Seeing her in action, I'm not surprised the supervisor became interested in her. Her general demeanour suggests to me that she is flirting, and I wonder if this had been her behaviour with her supervisor. Maybe that was the real reason he had wanted her out of his department. If so, she has wrecked his career.

'I can't thank you enough for your advice,' she murmured. 'Here is a cake I baked for you.' As she spoke, her crossed leg began to swing back and forth, as if giving her comfort, while her face flushed self-consciously as she handed him the parcel.

Dr White soon perceived that she wanted to linger to talk to him, but he was able to use his professional skill to usher her from his surgery without giving offence. He then dismissed her from his mind, at least for the moment.

Soon, however, he found his life plagued by her unsolicited attention. She began by ringing his surgery at frequent intervals during the day, and asking to speak to him. Finally, he had to tell his receptionist to stop putting her calls through to him. Sonja then began to ring his home in the evenings, but her calls were always answered by Dr White's wife. It was the calls after midnight that annoyed him most. Being the police doctor he was not able to turn his phone off.

Several weeks later he began to receive daily letters from Sonja to her 'darling doctor'.

When he mentioned his problem to several of his colleagues, he got no sympathy or advice. They simply reminded him that stalking was one of the hazards of medical practice. 'It happens to most of us,' they laughed. 'Just ignore her.' On another occasion he mentioned it to a police officer who often worked with him. 'Sounds like you are on to a good thing,' the officer replied with mocking amusement.

'Nobody treats this seriously,' Dr White complained ruefully to his wife. 'People are starting to suspect I am having an affair,' and he wondered if his wife was beginning to think likewise. For several months Sonja continued to make his life miserable, but he kept hoping that by ignoring her she would get the message and give up her amorous attentions.

Then, to his embarrassment, she would often wait for him to finish work, and accost him in the street as he walked to his car park. At times she would walk silently close behind him, or say, 'Your wife is a blood-sucker. She will take all your money now, and when you get old and frail and need her help, she will say "Get lost".'

This was of concern to Dr White, as he began to worry for his wife's safety. The next time she said it he stopped at the car park, and he turned to her saying, 'I gave you one piece of good advice that saved your job. My next piece of good advice is to take advantage of what I said. Go on your way and leave me alone. Never ever contact me or my family again.'

Sonja simply looked at him without saying a word, and stood watching him as he drove away.

Then, one evening police rang him to come and check out another body found in a city apartment. As usual, when he left the house, he carefully glanced around in case Sonja was lurking nearby, and he rapidly backed his car down the driveway. He had experienced several embarrassing episodes when she had followed his car as he drove to a night call. Although she never obtruded at his destination, she would often wait in the darkness, and follow him home again. But this night he drove to the scene without any sign of her. Her absence concerned him, as his wife was alone at home, and he worried what Sonja might get up to while he was away.

On his arrival several police met him at the door. 'We have pieced a few things together, doctor,' said a policewoman. 'It's a drug overdose in a woman aged twenty-four, who didn't turn up to work this morning. There are no signs of violence, and there is an empty drug bottle on the dresser.'

'Do we have a name?' asked Dr White.

'It's a Sonja Smith, and she left this note,' said the policewoman.

As she handed him a sheet of folded paper, Dr White's face blanched, and he hoped she did not notice the tremor of his hand as he reached for it. To escape attention he turned his back and unfolded the note.

My darling, it read. I was prepared to devote my whole life to make you happy, but you spurned me. Without you I can no longer go on.

With all my love, Sonja.

A policeman looked at Dr White, saying indignantly, 'Fancy treating such a pretty girl so shamefully. The bloke must have been a ratbag.'

'Yes, he must have been,' said Dr White sadly, but with guilty relief.

8

THE HAUNTING KISS

The memory of a kiss can last a lifetime.

It was little more than a momentary brushing of his lips across her cheek and mouth, but its memory would remain to haunt her.

It all began when she and her husband attended their annual conference ball. Early in the evening they met an out-of-town colleague and his wife who suggested they share a table. As they chatted and laughed, and with the wine beginning to loosen their inhibitions, she found herself becoming vaguely attracted to the colleague, who happened to be sitting directly opposite her. It wasn't his distinguished appearance that took her attention. Rather, it was in his ready wit and ease of conversation that she detected a man of culture; a lover of natural beauty; a sensitive man who aroused primitive desires behind her smiling eyes.

Eventually, out of politeness he asked her to dance. The request pleased her, but she was even more delighted to find him a polished dancer who held her in his arms until the music had finished. It was then, to her surprise, he bent and kissed her cheek. She had the distinct impression the contact of his lips was rather more prolonged than was the usually accepted social custom. As she jerked her head away their lips came in contact, and that illicit and stolen kiss sent a quiver of excitement through her.

As he escorted her back to her husband, it left her wondering if it had been accidental, or whether he had sensed a crackle of fire behind her bland expression; something for him to file away in his mind for future reference.

Throughout the evening, as they continued their reminiscing and joking, she would become aware of his eyes on her. It could have been a quite innocent look in the course of normal repartee. Still, each time she became conscious of his gaze it reminded her of the touch of their lips, and it left her pondering.

Over the weeks that followed, she often found herself recalling the excitement of the ball, as if this brief experience had woken some deep, vague yearning for something she could not explain. During her long, lonely evenings she would often sit listening to soft music while her husband was out at one of his interminable committee meetings. In these times of quiet solitude, the memory of the kiss would return unbidden, giving her comfort in its remembrance.

Formerly, she had always considered herself happily married, and enjoyed the daily routines of raising children and coping with the needs of a busy husband. In all the eleven years of her marriage she had appreciated the comfortable lifestyle her husband worked for. Now she was restless, and becoming disinterested in her daily chores.

For several years it was the memory of the kiss rather than the colleague that she would recall. Somehow it signalled to her that she could still be appreciated by a stranger. Confidence in herself slowly grew, giving her renewed interest in her appearance. Gradual changes in her personality transformed her into a more dynamic and charming woman. Her husband had become aware of subtle changes in her, but remained perplexed by them. At times he found her withdrawn and moody, at other times cheerful and winsome. Perhaps it's a sign of sexual frustration, he thought. I must admit in recent times I have eased off in that department. All these business worries have left me feeling rather jaded. From now on I must do better. She certainly enjoyed his renewed interest in her, responding to his advances to their mutual satisfaction.

As her self-confidence grew, her husband began to

notice her new pride in her appearance. Her updated interest in fashion found her elegantly dressed, wearing different make-up, and sporting a new hairstyle; all this time radiating an inner glow of wellbeing. Her husband began to see her as the vivacious woman he once married, and gave himself full credit for the change. She, however, did not know why she was different, but deep down her lingering memory of that half-forgotten kiss remained to allure her.

After several months she began to lose interest. Her husband soon noticed less response to his attentions, and on several occasions she frustrated him by rebuffing his advances. The frequency and intensity of their relationship slowly reverted to its previous pace. She did not find any particular problem with this, but her husband, who had been initiated into greater expectations, found the situation particularly irksome. He began to find fault in her in other ways, criticising her in small everyday activities, or perplexing her with occasional sarcastic remarks.

Soon she became aware that occasionally he would arrive home with the lingering smell of perfume about him, but at first dismissed any suspicion of his being unfaithful. One evening, however, the scent was so evident she mentioned it to him.

'Oh, that's just Stella,' he replied casually. 'She sat next to me at tonight's meeting.'

It was the same perfume she had noticed on him in the recent past, and she knew Stella used a different variety; besides, she rarely attended these meetings. It finally convinced her he was having an affair. An empty feeling of anguish welled up in her. Turning in despair, without a word, she left the room.

What had gone wrong? she wondered. She knew she had been a loving and faithful wife, caring for him as best she could. She knew she had worked hard and long with his welfare at heart, and giving him sons. In fact, she had given him the best years of her life. How could he be so selfish? She also knew that once love goes, it never comes back.

As time went by she was more frequently aware of perfume on his clothes, and in her anguish she did not know what to do. Soon he began to tell her of business meetings that on occasions would take him away for the weekend. 'I would take you along with me if it were not for the children,' he would tell her. On these occasions it was with a feeling of despair she would wave him off showing him a pleasant face. It was with nausea she would greet him back the next evening. Usually she would be in bed pretending to be asleep so she did not need to speak to him. But she found it increasingly difficult to be acting as if nothing was amiss.

Despite their relationship, she accompanied him to their next annual conference ball. At the gathering she posted herself where her husband's colleague could not fail to notice her in the crowd. He came across and met her as if by accident, and said 'Good evening'. After a few words of polite conversation he moved away leaving her strangely content.

At the next conference she failed to see him, and his absence made her aware that deep down she must have been looking forward to seeing him. His absence made her think of the man himself. She continued to feel unsettled for several weeks until one morning, as if the thought had just occurred to her, she mentioned, 'I didn't see your old colleague at the annual get-together this year.'

'Oh,' her husband replied, 'his wife died a couple of months ago, and I understand the poor chap is quite devastated. I heard it was some sort of cancer.'

The conversation left her saddened, and she was moved to write a letter of condolence to him. In his reply he mentioned he would be pleased to see her and her husband any time they passed his way. Their joint venture never eventuated because of their bickering, so that in time she became convinced that her husband was only waiting for some excuse to leave her.

Their separation came after an argument that began simply enough, but escalated into a shouting match that left them both exhausted. Her husband packed his bags and moved in with his mistress. With all the subsequent legalities settled, she and the children were left with the house, and enough maintenance to keep them debt free. She felt relieved, as if a heavy load had been lifted, and her naturally buoyant spirit returned with her new sense of freedom.

Now, in her moments of quiet solitude, memories of the kiss came into her mind more often, and the whispering voice of destiny turned her thoughts towards the possibility of life with her husband's colleague. The pleasant sensations this engendered initially gave her some satisfaction, but soon led to a restlessness, as fingers of enchantment sparked a desire to see him again. She toyed with the temptation for some time, knowing that in the end she would yield to its fascination.

Eventually, gathering her courage, she set out driving all through the day, and late in the afternoon reaching the town where he lived.

'I'm passing through,' she told him on the phone. 'I'm spending the night at the Regent Hotel. Would it be convenient for you to drop by for a cup of coffee in the lounge … for old times' sake?'

'Even better,' he replied enthusiastically, 'we would be delighted to see you at our place.'

We … We would be delighted … at our place. Her heart sank as she heard the words.

Meeting her at the door, and with a show of affection, he gave her a brief hug and firm kiss on the cheek, so unlike the subtle brush of his lips she remembered from the past.

'Come in and meet Judy; she is keen to see you,' he remarked warmly as he ushered her through the door.

An uneasy feeling came over her as he escorted her along the hallway, but she was astounded when she saw the new woman in his life. As they entered the room a rather short, stout woman rose to meet them. She wore harsh make-up, and her frizzed hair suggested a bad home perm. Her ample bust seemed to swell up from the neckline of her floral dress, to rise and fall with each raspy breath.

'Judy has been a friend of the family for many years,' he said. 'Now, since the loss of my dear Jenny, she has saved me from a miserable and lonely existence.'

She heard his words with dismay, and it set her mind thrumming through her recent past. She suddenly realised she had been the cause of all her trouble. It was really me who wrecked our marriage, and it has taken this visit to bring me to my senses. I feel so ashamed and foolish. She did not stay long. After a cup of tea and a few pleasant words she rose with some disquiet, determined to drive all the way home again at once.

As he escorted her out to her car she found the colleague rather quiet until he said, 'Until this evening I was unaware of your divorce. Now I can see a reason for your visit.'

'Oh, don't humiliate me,' she answered in a weak voice.

'On the contrary,' he replied. 'There is nothing permanent between Judy and me. We are simply helping each other through a bad patch. We will soon be going our own ways again, and still remaining friends. In the not too distant future, if you were willing, I would love to see you again and let our relationship develop.'

Later, as she tried to sleep, tears of joy streamed down through her half-closed eyelids.

9

THE HUMAN FACTOR

It is not us, but Nature that holds the key to our destiny.

Giving a smile of relief, Brenda closed the door behind her family as they left for work, and leaving her free to organise her day. Having raised two children and with a husband almost as demanding, she found a refreshing stimulus in her new independence. Deeply aware of the immorality of wasting her talents, she had kept herself busy with a variety of charity works for almost two years. At first she imagined her old degree in psychology would be put to good use, but soon found her atrophied knowledge irrelevant in the hurly-burly of everyday experiences.

While helping at a women's refuge, she heard disturbing stories of family violence and saw its results.

Still, she considered her finest contributions were as a Lifeline counsellor. At first, this responsibility overwhelmed her, leaving her feeling like a child about to take its first steps into an adult world. Giving advice to the unemployed, counselling the bereaved or those on the verge of suicide was all a new and worrying experience. With time came confidence, and she began to feel useful.

Now, with her family off her hands for the day, she checked her diary for the day's appointments. At 11 a.m. she would draw on her Lifeline experiences to speak on patterns of drug abuse. Later in the day she would attend a meeting about reorganising health services where she would give them the full blast of her concerns.

She decided it would be a day to be formal, and laid out clothes of feminine efficiency: a silk charcoal pantsuit, a white blouse, and red accessories. Then, with a sense of wellbeing she stripped and studied her reflection in the mirror. Apart from a few lines of maturity spreading from the corner of her eyes, she was well satisfied with what she saw. She simply stood there for a few moments radiating a mature beauty from the happiness and satisfaction of her achievements. Then she stepped under the shower with a feeling of extravagant self-contentment.

As her fingers caressed the lather across her breast she suddenly became aware of a small lump, which for the moment she dismissed as just the bulge of an underlying rib. Then, as if by delayed reaction, a creepy feeling spread through her and she paused.

Oh no. It can't be. It must be a rib. With rising panic she palpated her breast again, this time more carefully, and to her dismay was left in no doubt. It was definitely a small lump. She comforted herself with the thought that it was probably a cyst, but with some concern she stepped out of the shower and dried herself without thinking to glance in the mirror.

She spent the day in a trance. Nothing seemed to register in her mind, and she tried to bolster her feelings with a false *joie de vivre*. During the evening her husband suspected something was troubling her.

'You don't seem your usual self,' he said.

'I found a small lump in my breast this morning, and I'm having it checked tomorrow,' she replied.

'At your age it's probably just a cyst, and nothing to worry about,' he said reassuringly, and returned to read his newspaper.

She hadn't visited a doctor since her children had been born almost twenty years before. It was an apprehensive journey to his surgery. Everything seemed depressed: the houses, the shops, the traffic. It all seemed dismal, yet she didn't feel ill. While sitting in the waiting room she felt fit and well, and began to wonder if she was making a fuss over nothing, and began to feel guilty in taking the doctor's time.

'It's quite mobile,' he told her after a hurried examination. 'It doesn't seem anything to worry about at present. Come back in three months.'

She left the surgery reassured, but couldn't help wondering whether she should have asked for further investigations. Then again, he didn't seem the type to appreciate suggestions about his job.

'How did it go?' her husband asked, as if he had suddenly remembered her doctor's visit.

'He told me it was not serious,' she replied, rather disappointed by his apparent lack of concern.

She realised slow changes are hard to detect, but she continued to examine herself each day. For some weeks she remained unsure of any change, but eventually began to suspect the lump was becoming less mobile. She thought it time to return for a further check. On this occasion she went direct to a specialist who did not disguise the serious nature of the lump. After all the appropriate tests had been carried out she returned to his office.

'After a course of radiotherapy we will have to remove your breast,' he explained.

Although she had prepared herself for the worst, his words shocked her and left her too overwhelmed to cry. For the rest of the day she remained indoors, her mind restless, apathetic and sad. Later, when she broke the news to her husband, he became sullen.

'Where do you have this operation?' he asked.

'At the Mater Hospital, as soon as the radiotherapy is complete. It will save waiting for a public hospital bed.'

'But you are going to cost us a lot of money. Surely you could wait a little longer for a public bed. Maybe you don't even need an operation at this time. Perhaps this surgeon is just after a big fee.'

Shocked by his callousness, she left the room without replying in case he noticed a tear escape down her cheek.

After her operation she became more relaxed, as the surgeon treated her with kindness and understanding. He explained what had happened, including the removing of glands in her armpit, and readily answered her questions. She felt comfortable with him and trusted his advice. But after her return home she sensed a vague feeling of isolation from her family, as if they were not sure how to empathise with her. During the day she felt as well as previously. With her special bra she looked as shapely as before the operation. But still it was there; something that isolated her from her family, something that set her apart. She was most aware of it during the long hours of darkness, as her husband slept at her side.

In the past he had cuddled and fondled her with gentle caresses, giving her a sense of wellbeing, and satisfaction in the fulfilment of their love. Now it was different. On the rare nights he approached her, he did not waste time on elaborate preliminaries, as though he found her physically unattractive. As the months passed she became aware that at times the family conversation would stop when she entered the room, as if they had been talking about her.

One day she became frightened by a feeling of breathlessness lasting for several hours, and leaving her rather shaken. As she sat thinking, it occurred to her she had been losing some of her energy over the previous weeks, and with it her enthusiasm. She decided it was time to return to her specialist. He ordered further tests and scans, which confirmed a spread of her cancer.

'We will have to start you on chemotherapy,' he told her. 'I'll refer you to the appropriate specialist.'

As treatment got under way she began to feel nauseated, and her hair started to fall out.

'The treatment seems worse than the condition itself,' her husband said. 'And the expenses of all those doctors!'

By this time she was beyond caring, although saddened by her husband's attitude.

'Poor Mum,' she heard her daughter say. 'I hope it doesn't run in the family.'

'With all these expenses, too,' her son answered. 'Dad made it clear to me we can't afford any holiday for a long time. He said Mum should have waited for a public hospital bed; then it would have all been free.'

Her husband, too, seemed more distant than ever. He seemed to resent the extra work she caused, and went about his tasks with graceless resolve. Perhaps, like all of us, he is in a state of shock, she thought. None of us know how we would react to an unexpected crisis.

As the weeks passed, her energy continued to wane. The slightest exertion left her breathless. A mild back pain she had accepted without complaint began to bore into her, increasing her suffering until controlled by more drugs. She could see the end of her days looming, and wished the day would soon arrive. She could manage through the daytime. It was the interminable hours of darkness with only fitful bursts of sleep that wore her down.

The ailing Brenda was aware that various relatives were beginning to arrive to pay their brief visit. Through the doorway she would see their smiles give way to respectable seriousness as they entered her room, perhaps suddenly conscious of their own mortality. When they saw her waxen face and smelt the distinct odour of the bedridden, Brenda could sense them thinking, It is she who is dying; I am thankful it is not me.

They would stand around the bed looking gloomily at their feet, not knowing what to say before hurriedly leaving. Outside the door her husband would stand silent, waiting for a suitable response. The women would briefly kiss his cheek and shed a tear. The men would say, 'George … it's all a sad affair,' and shake his hand. After a quick cup of tea the visitors always seemed glad to escape.

After they had left she would turn her face to the wall and ponder what it all meant. Why is life so senseless? What have I done to deserve this? I have always been a good wife and mother, and tried as best I could to help others. Now I am a burden to my family, and will die in agony. Sometimes she felt angry and cheated, while at other times a sense of loneliness would engulf her, even in the midst of her family. Resistance seemed impossible, and there seemed no escape from an incomprehensible and dreadful death.

One evening her daughter came into the bedroom flushed with excitement. 'I've just become engaged to Simon. Aren't you happy for us, Mother?'

Her mother rallied her strength to smile approval, and asked, 'Have you set a wedding date?'

'No, Mother, we have decided to wait a little while.' In moments she had left the room.

Her mother knew what they were waiting for, and hot tears streamed down her sallow cheeks.

One evening she became aware of increasing breathlessness so that she could scarcely move or turn in bed without gasping. Somehow, despite the pain, a calm enveloped her and she felt as though she was floating. She recognised the presence of her husband when he gently took her hand. She opened her eyes and tried to smile, but already the hard lines of suffering had faded from her face, and replaced by a dignified composure in features that no longer responded. Her breathing, almost imperceptible now, was interspersed with occasional shallow gasps until, after one last deep breath followed by a sigh, she remained quite still.

10

THE DREAMS OF ALWYN

Envy is an overwhelming emotion that can lead to dishonesty.

It can be difficult to pick a con agent, especially when they have false documents or photographs to back their story.

Many years ago my wife and I were studying in London. I was a young doctor living in at a large hospital with every second weekend free to come home. Then, quite unexpectedly, my wife, Margaret, was awarded a medical scholarship that was too important to refuse. Since it required attendance at the research unit every day, we had to employ a live-in nanny to take care of our three children. Coming from New Zealand, we decided to try for a compatriot, and I went to New Zealand House and placed an advertisement on their notice board.

I had barely returned home when the phone rang, and a voice said, 'My name is Alwyn Johnson, and I am just back from a trip to the Continent. I've had Karitane training with experience in child welfare.' It led me to believe she had years of experience with children.

We immediately engaged her, and met her shortly afterwards at the local railway station. She was a plain-looking woman in her thirties, and I was surprised she had no luggage with her. She explained it had been held up in transit.

Alwyn settled in without incident, and seemed to get on well with the children. She took them in a large pram whenever she went shopping at the local centre, and she made friends with our landlord who lived next door. From the kitchen window I would watch her play with the children on the back lawn. Wearing the same old grey smock, she would sit silently as they played together. She did not join in their activities, but sat passively, watching them, — or was she? I often noticed her gazing into the distance with glazed eyes, as if her thoughts were far from the activity around her.

One weekend, about a month later, I noticed her reading a medical dictionary. 'That's an unusual book to be looking at,' I remarked.

She looked up shyly, saying, 'Just refreshing my memory.'

'For child care?' I asked.

'I'm afraid I misled you when I applied for the job. I

am not really a Karitane-trained nurse. Actually, I have a PhD in child psychology.'

'So you're really a Doctor of Philosophy?'

'Well ... yes.' She flushed, and with downcast eyes, avoided my gaze.

'I don't understand,' I said. 'If you are a doctor, why would you spend your time being a nanny?'

After a pause, and in a rather quiet voice, she went on to say: 'It's a long story. My husband was in the air force, and was killed in a crash at Ohakea last year. It has been a difficult time for me, and I just had to get away. Living a quiet life here with the children, and with no difficult decisions to make, is doing me a world of good.'

We felt genuinely sorry for Alwyn, and didn't press for details, but treated her with kindness and sympathy. Our landlord also seemed to go out of his way to talk to her with compassion. When we told our friends of our good fortune in having a child psychologist as a nanny, they all agreed they would be watching our children to see how they turned out. At times, however, I would notice Alwyn nursing one of them with a cigarette hanging out of her mouth. We wondered about her, but assumed she was simply a bit depressed. Otherwise we had no reason to doubt her.

Over the following weeks she began to allude to a legacy she expected when her husband's will had been settled. Then, one weekend she announced she was expecting about one hundred and fifty thousand pounds to arrive in her bank account any day. She added she was looking forward to buying a car to use on her days off, but could not decide between a Bentley and a Rolls-Royce. Would we kindly give her advice on a choice of model? We were taken aback, and suggested a range of cheaper cars, but she remained adamant.

Several weeks later, and a few days before my weekend at home, my wife rang me to say Alwyn had told her the money had arrived, and she would like to meet me in the city to help her choose a car. I donned my best suit and met her at Berkeley Square late on the Friday afternoon.

I don't know what the salesman thought of us, but he would have been dealing with a well-dressed customer accompanied by a rather shabby woman with all the money. It was an education to watch the professional smoothness of a top-quality salesman selling a top-quality product. Within an hour Alwyn had written a cheque for £5,800 for a beautiful two-tone Rolls-Royce, and had received the parchment ownership papers with her name engraved in faultless copperplate writing.

'We don't advise you to drive the car away,' the salesman said. 'We recommend you take our owner-driver course before risking the London traffic. If you agree, we will supply a chauffeur for the weekend.'

Next morning, the chauffeur-driven Rolls-Royce arrived to take us on a trip to the South Coast. It was the opportunity for numerous photos of Alwyn and the car, Alwyn with the chauffeur, and all possible combinations. We never saw the car again.

'It is too big to garage locally,' she said. 'And I won't drive it far until I get more confidence.'

As the months passed, things kept moving for Alwyn. 'I have just been appointed to a lectureship at Truro University in Cornwall, starting next year,' she announced towards Christmas. 'Would you help me choose a house?'

Soon, bundled into a small hire-car we headed for Truro, and went straight to a real estate agent. By some apparently prearranged plan he took us to a quite picturesque manor house nestling at the end of a magnificent tree-lined driveway that opened to extensive lawns and gardens surrounding the house.

'Built in 1650,' the agent said with a flourish. 'And a rare bargain at only thirty thousand pounds.'

The agent used Alwyn's camera to take numerous photos of her in attractive sites. But as we trooped through the house, admiring the mullioned windows, the parquetry floors, panelled walls and large rooms, I became more and more uneasy about the whole deal, and wondered if the money had gone to her head.

'Why would you want to buy such a large house when you would be living here all alone?' I asked her.

'I've been given the right to treat private patients,' she answered rather glibly. 'And some of them will live in.'

Her reassurance did little to lessen my concerns,

especially when a few days later she showed us all the photos that had been taken. She now seemed well enough organised and ready to take up her Truro appointment when the university opened in the New Year.

After Christmas we invited several New Zealand friends to dinner. They had heard about Alwyn, and were keen to meet her. She came into the room for the introduction, but after a momentary pause, turned and rapidly left. When she did not appear for the meal I knocked on her door to be told she had a migraine, and would not be joining us.

Back in the dining room, one of the guests was rather quiet. 'I'm almost a hundred per cent sure I know Alwyn,' she said. 'We were at primary school together in Auckland. She later worked in a factory, and is definitely not a doctor. I know she never married, and so she could not have received a legacy from her husband's estate.'

We were stunned. Why would she deceive us? What would it gain her? The fag in the corner of her mouth started to make sense. And what of our frequent finding of drops of urine on the toilet seat: hardly evidence of culture. Then there was the mysterious disappearance of threepences from the Christmas pudding! Soon we had further evidence. Written on her shopping list was 'bunsh of carits' ... and her with a PhD!

It gave me courage to return to the Rolls-Royce

agent where I had the answer the moment I entered the showroom. The salesman froze in his steps, visibly blanching when he saw me.

'I was here about six months ago,' I began, but my opening remark was met with a cold stare. 'The lady who bought that car was our nanny. She told us she had come into a large inheritance. If she actually paid for the car, all is well, but if she didn't, it would explain her odd behaviour.'

The salesman looked me up and down in silence, and seemed about to turn and walk away when he paused.

'She wrote out a cheque in full payment for that car on the Friday afternoon,' he rasped out through clenched teeth. 'Then, at the weekend she put almost five hundred miles on the clock. On the Monday morning the cheque bounced. She had only twenty-seven pounds in her account! Now the car can't be sold as new,' he muttered in a voice trembling with emotion.

I came away feeling the whole affair could have almost cost him his job. The same evening I rang the estate agent at Truro.

'It's all very strange,' he said. 'At present her cheque is being held by a bank in London. They told me her account is quite small, but they understand she has modest accounts in other banks, one of which believes she is expecting a large sum of money to be transferred from New Zealand.'

'That's most unlikely to happen,' I told him.

Alwyn left us several weeks later, unaware of what we had learned, and I helped her carry several heavy suitcases to the station. Over the weeks that followed, the accounts Alwyn used to collect while we were away at work began to fill our mailbox. It seemed she owed hundreds of pounds for clothing she had brought home on approval from smart city stores, and never returned.

A month after she left I answered a knock at the door one evening. A smartly dressed woman and two men with ministerial collars stood outside.

'We have come to ask you about Alwyn Johnson,' one of the men said. 'She gave us your names as a reference.'

'She told us how she lived with you here, and you helped her to cope with the sad loss of her husband,' his companion added. 'She has applied to work overseas as a missionary. But although she is a very Christian lady, after what she has told us, we feel her expertise would be better suited in our Asian accounting section. We have come to ask if you felt her sufficiently recovered to work in the tropics.'

Knowing her expertise in accounting, I swallowed hard. 'What has she told you?' I asked.

'As you know,' one of them answered, 'her late husband had been a successful psychologist in Cornwall, and Alwyn always kept his business accounts. She has shown us photographs of their beautiful manor house and their lovely car. How tragic for her to lose it all when her husband passed away so suddenly. Now all she has left of those better days are her photos and house plans.

'Yes,' said the lady. 'It has been a sad time for such a good Christian lady. The Lord moves in mysterious ways.'

Well, I thought, the Lord is about to move again. Poor Alwyn indeed!

11

STOLEN LOVE

Boredom and sex are an eruptive mix.

Ever since her family had grown up and left home, Helen was increasingly aware that her happiness depended on more than a life of extravagant ease. Despite having every material possession a suburban wife could wish for, she had slowly become dissatisfied with herself and her surroundings, even with her husband whom she loved.

She often wondered how she could change her dull existence for the better. She would think, I've been locked into domesticity for so long looking after a family that no longer needs me; my mind has atrophied from all the years of uneventful living. Sometimes she became gloomy, as time slipped by, leaving memories as sterile as a dream. Only regrets remained. As day followed day bringing nothing, she could even retain a cleaning lady who came once a week to vacuum and clean the silver.

Moping about the house one morning she casually picked out a magazine from the rack and strolled out to the patio. She reclined comfortably on a deckchair, and listlessly turned over the fashion pages. Occasionally she would glance up to the flower garden, or watch the finches enjoying their birdbath on the lawn. It was then that a long-dormant solution came into her mind, and she wondered why it had not come to her sooner. It's all so simple, she thought. I used to show promise as an artist. I'll go back and take lessons to develop my latent talents. It will give me some purpose in life, and perhaps I'll make new friends.

It was a cultural shock to find herself in a painting class of about a dozen young, mainly unemployed people, all filling in time; people she had nothing in common with. Only one of her class was about her own age and, like her, he too seemed out of place. Under the circumstances it was only natural that they would recognise each other's presence, sometimes even sitting together during the morning tea breaks. It was there that they introduced themselves: Helen and Martin.

'Why are you doing this painting class?' she asked him with little interest in his answer.

'I was made redundant last year, and at my age it has been impossible to find work.'

'I'm sure that is only a matter of time,' Helen

answered with enough concern to look at him more closely. In his early fifties, she guessed from the slight greying at his temples, while his smooth features and lack of weathering suggested he had always worked indoors.

'I had to get away from the house during the day,' Martin said. 'Since I have been unemployed my wife has changed. She says she is tired of me being under her feet all the time, and criticises everything about me. I just had to find something to do.'

Helen looked at him with embarrassment, not knowing how to answer.

Towards the end of the course Martin asked her what she intended to do with her training.

'I hope to go off over the hills with my easel and paints,' she replied with a show of enthusiasm.

'That could be dangerous for a lone woman in this day and age,' he said. 'Would you mind if I worked nearby since we are both doing the same sort of painting?'

Helen remained silent for a while thinking about his offer. Finally she agreed, but without telling her husband, whom she knew would not understand. She decided Martin seemed harmless enough, but thoughtfully resolved to keep a small stick handy just in case.

Their first afternoon together was a great success; Helen in slacks, floral blouse, and a ridiculous broad-brimmed hat; Martin comfortable in jeans and open-neck shirt. The distant drone of a mob of sheep gave a semblance of life in the quiet rural setting, while the occasional bark of a dog suggested far-off activity in an otherwise peaceful landscape. Remote snowcapped peaks blushed pink in the afternoon sun, forming a background for the nearer rolling hills.

The two artists sat several metres apart, each wrapped in their individual thoughts, and concentrating on the task at hand. When they did communicate it was to briefly discuss how best to portray a nimbus cloud, or scattered light on the dappled shades of a mountainside. Helen sensed it would be an impertinence to discuss personal subjects when she believed Martin was nearby solely as a protection, and he was acting the complete gentleman.

They arranged to meet again on alternate afternoons, each driving separately to a prearranged area. Helen's husband could hear her humming about the house and was particularly pleased to see how she had blossomed with a return to her old vivacious personality. It was clear to him she had at last found a way to escape from her previous boring existence. He watched her paintings take shape and he continued to praise and encourage her.

Helen always looked forward to her afternoons of painting, and on occasions would secretly appraise Martin's masculinity. At times she even wondered what he would be like in bed. Martin soon sensed this apparent interest and began to steer conversation along more personal lines. As their mutual attraction grew, they spent less time painting.

As she lay in bed one morning, she was unexpectedly shaken by the thought it was Martin rather than painting that had become more important to her. It can't be, she thought. Middle-aged people don't just fall in love; surely you are past it. Still, it started her thinking of all the unfulfilled years with a bland husband who loved her to a well-worn pattern; showering her with material goods, but without insight into her emotional needs. Her better judgment told her she should break her association with Martin, but at the thought of it her resolve weakened.

When she met Martin later in the day he sensed her agitation. 'Come and sit with me on the hillside,' he suggested, and for the first time he took her hand. 'You seem so dejected. Something must be troubling you,' he said. A large tear welled up on her eyelid and slid down her cheek. Moments later when he took her in his arms, she did not resist. They did not paint that afternoon; passion in the sun leaving them both exhilarated and exhausted.

That evening Helen's mind was in a whirl of agitation, her thoughts returning to relive every single moment of the ecstasy of the afternoon. She revelled in the temptation of future meetings, at the same time guilty of the implications. Her husband noticed nothing of this, as he spent the evening watching the television.

As the weeks passed, her infatuation with Martin

deepened. She could think of little else but of spending time with him. Never had she felt so comfortable with anyone else before. Thoughts of his gentle touch and understanding nature filled her with apprehension at the thought of ever losing him.

They continued to meet on several afternoons each week, their motives far removed from painting, and without insight beyond the day. They would lie together shaded from the warm autumn sun, perhaps talking, but more often united in tender embraces. Helen no longer thought of it as stolen love, but fancied herself so much part of Martin that she felt no remorse. She would have an occasional twinge of guilt when her husband gave her a questioning look, and she wondered if he suspected anything, but dismissed it as a touch of conscience.

As autumn turned to winter, the days remained warm enough for them to continue their clandestine meetings in the seclusion of the countryside. With all thoughts of painting relegated to a forgotten past, they spent their few hours together enwrapped in an aura of infatuation, and at times in a passion of secret desires. They would part reluctantly with the promise of meeting again to re-enter their own private world of enchantment. Helen was aware of the risks they took, but her obsession with Martin continued to override her better judgment. She felt drawn towards him by a force greater than herself, as if intoxicated by a love she could no longer control.

Then it happened.

Spring had already begun to warm the air, and with the rebirth of new buds, birds had become skittish, fluttering and scuffling in search of a mate. On the patio Helen sat absorbed in contemplation, her mind constantly returning to the hillside where she and Martin had sat exchanging tender thoughts and making love, oblivious of all else. She felt a deep ache when she thought how much her love for Martin had filled her life, and how empty it would be without him. As she stirred in her chair, the harsh stridor of the telephone in the hall brought her back to reality.

'Helen, we are in big trouble.' Martin's voice sounded strained. 'My wife had us followed yesterday and photographed in some rather compromising situations.'

Helen suddenly felt weak, and a pain deep in her spread like a tight girdle stifling her breathing. 'Go on,' she gasped.

'My wife became suspicious when my painting did not progress, despite all those afternoons away,' said Martin. 'She had an investigator follow us and presented me with the evidence this morning.'

'I hope she hasn't told my husband,' muttered Helen with rising panic. 'What are we to do, Martin?'

'My wife has ordered me from the house. She wants me to leave town. I can't tell you what she thinks of you!'

'Do you want me to come with you, Martin?' asked

Helen, her voice sinking to a whisper, as if she was hearing someone else speaking the words.

'I can't ask you to come with me now. I have very little money. I will have to find somewhere else to live, probably in another town, but I will keep in touch.'

Helen put down the phone, hardly able to believe what she had just heard, but realising her quest for happiness had led her into a wretchedness of her own making.

She wandered back to the patio in a dejected way with a feeling of inner deadness that left her unable to think, or even notice surroundings that a few minutes before had given her so much pleasure. For several hours she sat despondently, as if in a trance. Occasionally she moved about the house in brief fits of agitation. Oblivious of the passing hours, she was roused from her lethargy by the sound of her husband's car in the driveway. He is home early … Surely he must know … Perhaps he is livid and will want to throw me out.

Moments later, with the rasp of a key in the lock, she stood silently across the room, her head bowed in shame, as if waiting for his anger to explode. Instead, for a moment, he looked pointedly at her. Then taking her in his arms, he held her close, but said nothing. Tilting her wan face towards him, he kissed her gently on her lips. She felt overwhelmed and powerless in his silence. But am I overreacting? she thought. He may be unaware of the situation, or at most only partly informed.

At last he said, 'It's a pleasant surprise to find you at home. Usually you are out painting when I am home early.' Helen remained uneasy, but concluded that if he knew anything, he did not wish to disrupt his own lifestyle by a confrontation.

One morning several weeks later, she received a phone call from Martin.

'I have found a place in Auckland,' he said in tones that left her doubtful of his intentions. 'We have become too far apart to meet,' adding huskily, 'Meantime we will have to lead our separate lives.' He did not ask her how she was coping.

Helen was stunned by his apparent coolness towards her, and struggled to suppress any latent hopes she held for him. He surely was not just using me, she kept thinking, or perhaps he is too ashamed to ask me to go to inadequate housing.

As the weeks turned into months and years, Helen's old yearning never left her. A ring on her phone would set her pulse racing, but it was never a call from Martin. Without any communication from him, time slowly blurred her yearning for him, but love's grief of old continued to embrace her. She could manage once more with normal living, except in moments of quiet solitude when her thoughts would drift back to him. When sitting in the sun she might feel a gentle touch on her shoulder. She would glance around, but nobody was there.

She wondered what he was doing, and if their time

of stolen passion still meant anything to him. She knew his Auckland address, but he had no phone number, and she was loath to write. In moments of self-pity she imagined him waiting for her. When she lived at such a great distance from him she had no excuse to visit him. But when her husband had an opportunity to attend an overseas conference several years later, it gave her ten days of freedom in which she succumbed to the temptation to see Martin once more.

After driving most of the day, she finally arrived at the broken-down Auckland suburb where Martin lived. She felt out of place driving around the back streets in her BMW. The old unkempt houses unsettled her, and raised her doubts about seeing Martin again. She stopped outside his run-down house. She paused for some time, her arms resting on the steering wheel and her head bowed. Then, in trepidation she walked to the door, wondering if Martin would be pleased to see her, or if he was living with another woman.

'Martin?' drawled a worn-out middle-aged woman who answered the door. 'He doesn't live here any more. He had a stroke about a year ago, and he went to a nursing home. Such a nice chap, too.'

Helen felt devastated, but eventually found the nursing home. Surely now he will be pleased to see me, she thought.

'Yes, he was here,' the woman in the office said. 'Unfortunately he died about three months ago ... Used to talk about someone called Helen ... If he had a restless night he would call her name.' Turning to resume work the woman paused, as if remembering something, before saying, 'He insisted on having a half-finished painting hanging above his bed, and saying it was his heaven and hell. It looks more like mountains to me. Take it if you like. It is no use to us here.'

Helen managed to control her anguish until she had the painting in her car. She did not drive away at once, but sat thinking. As she gazed at Martin's painting, its half-finished scene triggered memories of their old passion and stolen love. Her pulse began to pound and her breathing quickened. Tears wet her eyelids and dropped onto the painting. As she continued to gaze she realised if she took it home, as she was tempted to do, she would have to hide it from her husband, and look at it in secret. Each time she looked at it these same emotions would return to upset her, and remind her of her stolen passion. She would never get closure. But if she discarded the painting, it would surely bring closure to her long-standing heartache.

As she drove home pondering what to do, a peaceful change seemed to engulf her.

On a sudden impulse, she stopped at a building site and deposited Martin's painting in a rubbish skip. She drove on with a relaxed feeling that her long saga had reached its conclusion, and with time, closure would bring her peace.

THE DOCTOR'S TALE

Things are not always what they may seem.

As Prue clicked the surgery door shut behind her, she instinctively discarded her role of family doctor to welcome a return to the more womanly instincts of her recent marriage. She had just finished her weekly evening surgery at the end of a long day; not without its moments in giving advice to a constant stream of patients. But now she was contemplating the quiet sanctum of home, and the passionate arms of her new husband of six months. She knew he would be waiting for her patiently.

With his conventional nine-to-five job in the Justice Department, she knew that these long and lonely nights could not be much fun for him. Poor George, how could he understand all I have to do? she thought, as she walked to the darkened car park. As for me, I have to be two people: a housewife with all its chores, and at the same time a doctor with time not my own. It's a narrow path to tread.

She recalled some of society's miscellany she had seen during the day, and wondered how some people manage to cope with the hurly-burly of modern living. There had been that young country girl who had asked for a prescription for Kodachrome after some wag had convinced her it was the latest birth control pill. And Prue laughed as she recalled the elegantly dressed matron who complained to her in all seriousness that watching television for more than a few minutes gave her a pain in the balls; the temporary impasse being resolved when the woman pointed to her eyeballs. Prue never ceased to wonder at what some people would tell her in the privacy of her consulting room.

As she drove home she put memories of the day aside and surrendered to the autumn night. The air seemed to glimmer under a naked moon rising behind diaphanous trees along the roadside. A perfect night for romance, she thought. As she turned into her driveway the light on her porch flashed on and the door opened to reveal her husband whose long wait had been a sauce to his expectations. Prue gave a smile, as she recognised his covert passions.

After a hurried supper, which she suspected was too lengthy for him, he took her in his arms with the suggestion of having an early night.

'An early night, George?' she laughed. 'It is already

after ten o'clock.' But she did not resist. Arm in arm they dallied flirtatiously along the hallway and into the bedroom where Prue allowed him to remove her elegant clothes of professional respectability. He hastened to snuggle into bed beside her when their sanctity was shattered by the sounds of her emergency home phone.

'Oh, can you come quickly, doctor … it's our baby … he has swallowed our condom!'

As the words of the caller tumbled out, Prue saw her husband turn his back in exasperation, and cover his head with the sheet. After explaining the problem to him Prue scrambled out of bed to dress in slacks and loose sweater before kissing her disappointed husband a fond *au revoir*.

'Do you really have to go?' her disgruntled spouse asked hopefully. 'Surely the crisis will pass!' he added, joking through clenched teeth. His forlorn expression left her with a feeling of remorse, but she knew where her responsibilities lay.

As she left the house, she found the evening air had become cold. And with dew beginning to freeze on the grass, she shivered as her chilled fingers fumbled to open the garage door. Everything seemed dismal to her as she backed her car down the darkened driveway. Even the moon had vanished behind louring clouds.

She was about to drive away when she saw her front door fly open. She was astounded to see the naked figure of her husband waving to her in the light of the hallway. As she paused, he came running towards her, barefooted across the frozen lawn.

'Your after-hours phone is ringing again, Prue,' he shouted. 'You had better do both calls while you are out.'

Prue sprang out of her car and hurried back to the telephone before it stopped ringing. To her surprise it was the voice of her previous caller. As she listened, she glanced at George standing beside her shivering with the cold, and she began to giggle. He wondered if it was his lack of attire, or whether it was something the caller was telling her. As she hung up, Prue looked at him with a twinkle in her eyes.

'I don't have to go out, after all,' she said with a laugh. 'The man said everything is all right again, and they don't need me.'

'But why?' asked her husband, beginning to look more cheerful.

'Oh, it's simply because they have found another condom!'

13

A TOUCH OF THE GODDESS

An ambitious person remains focussed on one goal. All other choices remain secondary.

Carol was aware something unsettling was happening to her, and not sure she approved. She had thought herself to be a successful executive, happy in her work, and in complete control of herself and her future. Then seven months ago *he* burst into her life. Now, thoughts of him seemed to be there, lurking in the back of her mind; ready to appear without bidding, ready to confound her with his image. Her attraction began slowly over the weeks and months as they worked together on several projects and interfered with the smooth running of her affairs. As a manager of a large tourist company, he first appeared at her office to discuss group travel arrangements for a conference, and her discussions with him had been a new experience. His charm in several follow-up projects had turned everything topsy-turvy for her.

In the past she had become disillusioned in her dealings with men. Anything outside their immediate interests had left them tongue-tied, or bluffing. Their rather inept and clumsy lovemaking, too, had been equally unimpressive. Either way, she had found male company boring. It left her wondering if she expected too much, or had chosen badly.

When talking with married women over the years, the subject of men would have occasionally arisen. But their unsolicited comments had decided her against risking an unfulfilled life in the suburbs with some dull man who had once taken her fancy. She had opted to put marriage on hold, and set out to qualify in commerce and business management. By the age of thirty-two she had built up a secure and rewarding life as an executive.

Now she had a dilemma. Unlike her previous male friends, she had found Mark delightful company on the occasions they had been together, and in his work he seemed to have travelled everywhere. In their business discussions she had found him sympathetic to many of the projects that took her interests. This empathy with him was beginning to sound alarm bells with her emotions.

She was still uncertain of Mark's feelings towards her, but he seemed to be going out of his way to be friendly. She suspected he might have been waiting for her to finish work, because a week ago he had met her as if by accident as she left her office for the day. It was then that he invited her for a cup of coffee. It would have been easy to fob him off, but she looked up and saw his earnest expression, and laughed, 'Why not?'

As they sat across the coffee table she learned a little about him; how his wife had left him, and now after two years he had at last come to his senses, and put past regrets behind him.

'I never expected to feel so comfortable in the company of a career woman,' he added with a blush. 'I have been wondering if you happened to be free at the weekend? We could have a drive into the country.'

Carol hesitated. Involvement with Mark at this stage could affect her career. On the other hand, she felt drawn to him.

'I have inherited a small country property,' Mark said. 'It's too small to be farmed, and a little too far from the city to commute each day. Still, it is a pretty spot with a patch of native bush, lots of birds and a little stream. It's an ideal retreat for us to picnic in.'

'Put in that way, how could I refuse?' Carol said, with the hope she was not about to take her first step into an unmarked minefield. Despite this, she remained on tenterhooks in anticipation of the day.

At first light on that morning she began to stir in the warmth of her bed. In her half-wakening state her mind turned to Mark and his visit later that morning. As she rose and laid out her clothes, her inner turmoil grew as she realised how much Mark had come to mean to her. For years she had lived alone in her apartment, preferring a career and personal achievements. She did not consider that loving somebody could complete and fulfil her life.

After showering and an application of suitable body perfume, she dressed in a flowing skirt of olive green, and a multicoloured blouse, the reds, greens and yellows reflecting the agitation in her mind. She spent considerable time trying a variety of hairstyles until finally framing her face with her loose black curls secured at the temples with jet combs. Her normally high self-esteem was somewhat shattered when she studied her mirrored reflection. Flushed cheeks betrayed her excitement. It was not the image she had planned to project. But there was still an hour to regain an air of sophistication before Mark's arrival. Making herself comfortable on her couch, she relaxed with lids closed to listen to the restful music of *Spiegel im Spiegel*.

As she quietly absorbed the music, her mind kept drifting back to Mark. Here I am, she thought. After all my spadework I've settled into a successful career with bright prospects. Now, I have let him come uninvited into my private world. At present the two will not mix. I must take my time.

Her musings were interrupted by Mark's ringing of her doorbell. As she rose to answer, she felt her pulse leap, and her whole body seemed sensitised and glowing warm from some source deep within her. Her legs were jelly, and she noticed her hands tremble slightly as she straightened her skirt.

After a hurried appraisal of her appearance she opened the door to find a smiling Mark holding a large bunch of roses. With a mock gesture he thrust them forward saying, 'Just a silent token, but one that expresses my feelings more adequately than me.'

'How beautiful,' laughed Carol, wondering if he had been quoting. But her downcast eyes told him she was duly impressed. 'Come in while I arrange them,' she added. She was quick to notice his designer trousers did nothing to distract from a lithe muscularity, while his open-neck shirt did justice to his well-developed chest.

'I can see you have an artist's eye,' he said, as she arranged the flowers to show them to their best advantage.

As they turned to leave, Carol glanced back at the roses and sensed her attraction to Mark was getting out of control. Later, seated next to him in the car, her emotions settled as she relaxed in his company. She so enjoyed their conversation she was surprised to find they were soon at their destination.'

'It's more beautiful than I had imagined,' she exclaimed, as she opened the car door. Then, with a glow of excitement she ran off through the long grass with a laughing Mark in eager pursuit. For a while they gambolled about the hillside like two children, until Mark suggested he show her around the bush-clad slopes. Once in the shade of the trees, Mark reached for her hand to lead her through the dank undergrowth, but somehow the coolness of the air brought Carol partly back to her senses.

After strolling hand in hand through the trees, they came to a small clearing beside a little stream. 'Just the place to lay out our picnic gear,' said Mark, who clearly had been there in the past. As he prepared the site, Carol sat nearby, looking up at the patches of blue sky between the branches. In the quiet surroundings, she listened to the faint sounds of the breeze as it caressed the leaves above them.

As if reading her thoughts, Mark said, 'Listen to the rustling of the leaves. The trees must be whispering to each other of our new-found love.'

It was the first time she had heard him mention the word 'love', but she closed her eyes and said nothing. Soon she felt the light caress of his lips on her cheek, but she continued to lie there silently. When she felt his touch on her bare shoulder she stirred and asked rather unconvincingly, 'What are you doing?'

Mark looked at her intently, as if studying her features, and after a pause, whispered, 'In my travels I have often been moved by the beauty of all those ancient Greek statues of gods and goddesses, but here beside me is the real thing. Carol, you put all these great works of art to shame. You are a real live goddess. Can you blame me for touching?'

Carol began to sit up, and suddenly Mark's arms

were around her. She felt his impassioned kisses on her shoulders and neck, and as his mouth pressed fervently against hers she felt resistance fade. Later, with the contact of his smooth skin against her she soared to new heights of emotion. Locked in each other's arms, great waves of ecstasy spread through her with an intensity she had never known, until at last they lay relaxed in each other's arms.

As the afternoon wore on a strange feeling of dejection seemed to engulf her, and she murmured, 'Let us get dressed and leave.' She felt ashamed and awkward, and noticed Mark was unusually quiet. Anything they said sounded stilted and formal, as if a barrier had come between them.

How like the Garden of Eden, thought Carol. This morning we were happy together and our emerging love for each other seemed so pure. Now after tasting the forbidden fruit we have become like strangers in each other's presence.

On the way home it occurred to Carol that Mark had behaved in a very experienced way. It set her wondering how many other women he might have taken to his country property. Does he think of me as just another conquest?

Arriving at her apartment, Mark escorted her to her door in a solemn manner. After a brief embrace Carol suggested, 'Perhaps we should have a cup of coffee together.' Mark followed her into the lounge, but when she saw the roses so lovingly arranged that morning, hot tears welled up and flowed unrestrained down her cheeks. Carol felt Mark's arms embrace her as he cradled her against his chest.

When Carol had regained her composure, she found Mark looking straight at her. As their eyes met, he murmured, 'If our day together had meant nothing more than two busy people having a good time, it could be written off as just a great experience, and easily forgotten. But Carol, I believe our relationship goes much deeper. It means so much more to us because I have realised we are both in love.'

Carol continued to look at Mark, who went on to say, 'I know that is why we have become embarrassed in each other's company.' With his words he felt the stiffness relax in her body. As she withdrew from his embrace, he added, 'I have been surprised, too, and concerned by the intensity of our emotions today.' Carol motioned him to a chair, and poured the coffee.

'I also know,' Mark continued, 'how involved you have been in building a successful career, but life demands more than hard work. Carol, think how earnestly you have aspired to building your reputation to the neglect of your true happiness.'

'But I have been very happy until today,' she answered. 'I have always trusted myself, but now I'm not so sure. We must not repeat today's mistakes; possibly even parting company.'

At the thought of parting company Mark looked mournfully at her, and seemed lost for words. Then after a long pause he burst out hopefully, 'Carol, I cannot lose you now. I know it is the wrong time to tell you this, but I find myself so much in love with you. I must see you again.' Then after a deep breath he whispered, 'Carol, I also know it is the wrong time to ask, but will you marry me?'

From that moment Carol knew she had the situation under control, and said, 'For the present, let us just be good friends, and perhaps you will ask me again in the future. I never do things by halves. It is all or nothing for me. I still have more to accomplish in my career before I devote myself to a married life. Let us wait until we are free to pledge ourselves to each other.'

'You can depend on me to treat you with the respect you deserve,' Mark said with a smile. 'Now let us enjoy that cup of coffee together.' After a pleasant chat he rose, and reaching for her hand he brought it to his lips. Moments later his arms went around her in a brief hug. As he left he turned at the door, and giving a gracious bow, said, 'Until we meet again.' In moments he was gone.

As Carol stood in silent thought her eyes caught sight of the flowers she had so lovingly arranged that morning. She was about to throw them out when she hesitated. No, she thought. I'll leave them as a reminder of this important day in my life.

14

JOURNEY INTO FOLLY

*Parents can do little more than set their children a good
example. It is up to the child to accept it, or not.*

With mounting anticipation Marcia strolled across to join the man waiting nearby.

'You will find the Gathering a welcoming place to live,' he said, as he escorted her to his well-polished utility van. 'I'll show you around, and introduce you to the others when we get there. We are always pleased to meet new members of our group. It is only a short drive across town and along the river.'

Marcia felt a spreading glow of excitement as the man, who called himself Clive, murmured on in his insipid tone. As he drove, she was able to study his wind-flushed face, bland from years of uneventful living. In his mid-thirties, she thought. And she was quick to notice the fine purple venules webbed across his cheeks and nose, and recognised his obvious alcoholic background.

'You will probably find it will take you several days to adjust to the routine,' Clive said. 'You can't change overnight from being a university student to a caregiving fieldworker.'

'Well, I want to do something more useful with my life,' Marcia said. 'I have found good friends in the outside world. I know my parents would never approve of them, or of what I am doing now, but we care for those around us, and we don't mess up the environment.'

'Those are worthy thoughts,' said Clive.

'So what do we do all day?' she asked, as if to confirm what she already knew.

'Well, you and the other ladies work in the vegetable gardens so we can be self-sufficient. The men go begging. There is a lot of money to be had in begging if you do it right. And we've got it all worked out to help others. But don't forget to register with the Social Welfare Department because the money is always helpful through lean times.'

She liked it when he used the word 'ladies'. To be referred to as one of the girls always seemed a put-down, and made her angry.

'Is there any drinking at the Gathering?' she asked casually.

'Not much,' he said. 'It's frowned on by common consent. All our important decisions are mutual.'

'What about drugs?' she asked.

'We have several sources of supply,' he said. 'Sitting for hours begging can become boring, and a small dose now and then relieves the monotony. Of course, it is always available at the Gathering to any of us.'

Marcia remained silent as she assessed his remarks.

'We are one big family here at the Gathering,' Clive continued enthusiastically. 'The desire to help others is in everybody here. But out in this world, where plenty abounds, people are not generous. Begging is not very profitable in the rich suburbs.'

'I have heard it said that you practise free love here,' Marcia said in a hushed voice, as they entered the Gathering site.

'We share not only our work, as you can see all around you, but also our whole psyche, each with the others. Some couples continue living in harmony for much longer than others who unite and part without animosity: like atoms in nature.'

Clearly, I am about to learn a few graphic lessons, Marcia thought, as she arrived to a welcoming crowd. I'm glad I took the precaution of starting the pill.

The next morning found her at work in the vegetable patch. At first she felt a sense of resentment having to share her personal things with all the others. But this shock to her upbringing soon recovered, as she hoed between the rows of carrots with all her youthful enthusiasm. She began to enjoy the company of her new-found friends, and considered the dirt on her hands a bonus for her efforts.

For several days she worked intently, waking each morning in her little cottage eager to begin the new day. One afternoon she noticed her companions quietly drifting away one or two at a time to other areas of the gardens until she was left working beside a young man not much older than herself. She had noticed him that morning climbing into the begging van with others to do the morning begging shift. Now, later in the afternoon he was free to work in the gardens.

'Here is a pair of gloves for you,' he said in shy tones baited with sincerity. 'It would be a shame to see those soft hands spoiled.'

She registered his friendly smile, and realised that like the others, he seemed to have her interests at heart. As she continued to hoe, she gave him a subtle appraisal in a basic feminine manner. A shock of fair hair hung across his forehead, and his bare arms bronzed by the sun suggested a strength that somehow excited her. She sensed his eyes searching her, as if the object of secret dreams. Suddenly she knew this would be the man she would come to live with.

He introduced himself as Tom, and in the days that followed, their friendship grew. Soon she found that each morning when she awoke, it was Tom she wished to see. Then one afternoon he said, 'I think we should spend more time together.'

'I would like that,' she heard herself saying. 'I'll prepare a meal for us tonight.'

Filled with new enchantment, they began living together. Marcia's previous shallow experience was soon relegated to a trough of forgotten memories, as passions stronger than herself drew her to Tom. Each day his kisses gave her a longing for pleasures more intense. Time passed like a dream, as she felt herself at the threshold of a marvellous world of ecstasy where her previous existence was far away. Love had intoxicated her, and was becoming indispensable.

Marcia had never felt so committed to another as day followed day, bringing new happiness. Each day, when Tom returned from begging, they worked together in the fields or milked the cows. In the evenings they set up house in an old cottage at the Gathering. The nights brought sensations she had never dreamed of, and in her mind she began to dress Tom in heroic vestments. The grey walls of their drab cottage became a mansion that housed her dearest fantasies.

She had never been happier as she took her first steps into a relationship that gave her so much primitive excitement. They lived together, laughed together, and loved together in a world where ordinary existence was far away. When his frequent embraces hindered her movements she laughingly teased him while her eyes asked for more. He laughed good-naturedly at her cooking failures, but enjoyed the meals because it was she who had made them. They lived in an enchanted world of joy and affection, oblivious of all else. She was a woman in love, and standing in his aura. She readily agreed to his wishes, as desires clouded her reason, and her face was beginning to glow with the indefinable beauty of fulfilment.

They shared their idyllic existence all through the summer and into autumn before she began to wonder if Tom's ardour was beginning to wane. It started in small ways, leaving her uncertain. He seemed to listen to her with the required etiquette, but at times she sensed his thoughts lay elsewhere. At times she would make a pointed remark in the hopeful expectation of his agreement. She would say, 'Our love is made in heaven' or 'Our love is more binding than steel bands. Nothing can break it.'

Usually he would look towards her and say nothing. Although she found his lack of eye contact unsettling, she hoped it was just a passing cloud. But somewhere deep in her she sensed he was losing interest in her. At times she became morose and uncommunicative, dissatisfied with everything, and in particular with Tom.

As stress began to distort her mind, horrible suspicions began to crowd her thoughts. Who else in the Gathering had already lived with Tom, and was perhaps even now quietly observing her, waiting to see how long his relationship would last this time. Her attitude soon affected Tom, who began to fail in his ultimate acts of love. It left her in a pitch of high excitement and unable to sleep. Their association had begun to show its first rift.

This ruthless current of suspicion left her happiness in tatters. Days that once flashed by in the heat of passion now seemed much longer, and she felt the warm glow of her feelings being slowly crushed. By now, the wet winds of autumn had left a patina of bronzed leaves scattered on the muddied garden, and with winter approaching they began to spend more time indoors: Tom with his carving; Marcia with her weaving.

In her time of trial, Marcia knew that Tom could not be seeing anyone else, yet he had become distant, as if tiring of the eternal monotony of passion. Often she would look across at him in silence, seeking some sign of the affection she hoped he still felt for her. Occasionally a tear would pearl down her cheek when he gave her a honeyed but ambiguous smile that left her unsure of his love.

Her state of uncertainty continued through winter, but with the approach of spring some invisible change seemed to bring her to her senses. She concluded if Tom had ever loved her, he no longer did with the ardour that once stirred him. The constant drumming of rain on the roof depressed her, and she worried that the time was approaching when, like others at the Gathering, he would drift to another partner. By now all fun had left Tom, as he met each day with a gloomy pleasure that left her feeling wretched in loving a man who no longer cared.

With the onset of spring the people of the Gathering took on a fresh liveliness. They emerged from their shelters to prepare the new season's plantings. The men sat about in groups discussing new ways of begging and how to avoid spring showers. Outdoor activities brought Marcia back into contact with all her new-found friends again. She felt a curtained sense of self-consciousness in their presence, and wondered if they noticed if Tom was already bored with her. She had imagined her days of love would stretch on through the years, but felt awkward now, and hoped her unhappiness did not show.

Invigorated by the warming afternoon sun, Tom worked with diligence. Lacking his romantic conversations from the past, he would notice Marcia's close proximity with an air of resigned acceptance, and converse in tones of strained courtesy. It soon became obvious to their friends that the romance was finished. Marcia, however, continued to hope it was all just a temporary lack of empathy, and refused to accept their intolerable situation.

Tom, on the other hand, was learning that partners could easily be acquired, but hard to get rid of. He found great difficulty in coping with a tearful woman who did not accept his rebuffs with the equanimity of his former partners, and Marcia was a young woman used to having her own way. He had misjudged the white heat of her smouldering volcanic core, and did not know how to handle the enigma. When in a pleading voice she tumbled out her love for him, he could never think of a fitting reply, and just looked at her with animal muteness. He was fearful of taking her in his arms out of pity lest she misunderstood.

One afternoon, Marcia looked up from her hoeing to see Tom in earnest conversation with a girl who had arrived at the Gathering during the winter. She could tell they were openly flirting, the girl looking at Tom with a yielding tenderness he was obviously enjoying.

The pain of sudden jealousy almost caused Marcia to cry out, as she threw her hoe to the ground and stumped angrily back to the cottage. Hot tears of mortification burned down her face as she threw herself onto the bed and covered her head with a pillow. Marcia knew their relationship was over and, for the moment, she just wanted to be alone.

Tom, who had noticed the incident, did not hurry off to appease her, but continued working. Although he was thinking of leaving her, he did not relish a scene in front of the Gathering. He decided it was the opportunity to move out and start living with his new partner. He did not return to Marcia for his evening meal, but left her to simmer down.

The next morning when he returned to the cottage to collect his belongings he found Marcia lying motionless in bed. Her stertorous breathing suggested to him that she had taken an overdose of drugs, which her tiny unresponsive pupils confirmed. Tom called the alarm, and as he and his panic-stricken friends rushed her to hospital, he could see the shadow of another world looming in her glazed eyes. He stayed near her bedside for several hours as doctors worked on her, but when her parents arrived he soon took the opportunity to flee back to the Gathering.

Late in the day Marcia began to awaken. The sound of her mother's voice seemed to stir her to open her eyes. As she struggled to discover where she was, her sallow face showed a strange haunted look in the subdued lighting of the ward.

'You are all right now, Marcia,' her mother said, and when she was fully awake, added, 'You have been through a most harrowing time. Your new-found friends have treated you most unfairly. I had a short talk with Tom before he left. It seems that although your association may have given you a brief time of happiness, it was built on very flimsy grounds. When you are ready to come home you will find all the love you need with the family.'

Marcia smiled again. 'Mother, I have come to my senses at last. I am looking forward to coming home and being with my family again. Tom was my golden idol, but now I realise he is just gilded clay.'

15

THE POWER OF ROMANCE

Love is a many-splendoured thing.

It was 1945, and the war in Europe was drawing to a close. As the Allies advanced into Northern Italy it brought the New Zealand forces in line to capture Venice, prompting the New Zealand Commander-in-Chief to issue an order. In effect, it advised the New Zealand forces to capture the Hotel Danieli near the centre of Venice, and hold it against all other forces. This hotel was among the top six in the world, and in the past, the commander had spent his honeymoon there. Now he wanted it for New Zealand forces after the war.

Several weeks later, with peace declared, I arrived at the hotel late one morning to stay for a few days. After lunch I set out sightseeing. A couple of foot-weary hours later I was making my way back to the hotel when I came upon a NAAFI run by the British Army, and where I could get a cup of tea and a biscuit. I found the dining room packed with British soldiers plus a queue waiting for tables. But across the room I noticed a table for three set against a far wall. Two of the chairs were taken by women in British battle dress, and one chair remained empty. I strolled across.

'Is this chair available?' I asked.

'Yes, come and sit with us,' one of them said.

'I'm surprised to see an empty chair with all these battle-hardened troops here,' I said.

'Oh, they are all too shy,' they replied with a laugh.

This set the ball of happy chit-chat rolling, and in the course of the next twenty minutes we were engaged in pleasant conversation. Then the blonde one stood up saying, 'I am on duty tonight, and I'll have to catch the shuttle bus.' Within a few moments she was gone, leaving me with the other woman, named Vera. She naively mentioned she did not have to return until 10 p.m. I got the message!

'What are you doing out here in Italy getting yourself bombed?' I asked. She went on to tell me her life story.

'I grew up in the coal dust of a mining town in the north of England before being called up for war service,' she said. As she talked on, her life seemed to have no fairy-tale content, only ugly years of grime, coal dust, and wartime bombings. Now she was camped miles away at the edge of town.

'It is very inconvenient for you having to stay so far away,' I said.

'Ordinary ranks have to take what is given to them,' she replied.

'I am an ordinary rank, too,' I said. 'But my hotel is first class, and is in walking distance.'

'I don't believe you,' she said. 'You are having me on. Ordinary ranks don't get fancy hotels.'

After talking about the hotel for several minutes, I said, 'Well, come and see it. It is only a short walk away.'

'I still think you are having me on,' she said, as we left the NAAFI together. After a pleasant stroll through the Venetian streets, we rounded the Ducal Palace corner, and approached the hotel.

'That red building ahead is the hotel,' I said. 'You can see ordinary ranks coming and going.'

'I still think you are joking,' she said, but with less confidence in her voice.

When we entered the foyer she stopped and glanced about. As she took in the scene her jaw dropped and she stood transfixed: Chinese silk replacing wallpaper, chairs with the sheen of rich velvet, old masters hanging on the walls, a string quartet playing in a nearby alcove, and hordes of ordinary ranks coming and going with not an officer in sight. Vera was clearly overwhelmed and stood in silence, as if her mind had gone blank. Finally she looked at me and whispered, 'I never knew such luxury existed.'

'Come and listen to the music,' I said, and led her to a comfortable velvet-covered chair nearby.

'I have sometimes heard beautiful music like this on the radio,' Vera said. 'It always draws my mind away from the roughness of my everyday life, and gives me a feeling of a purity I find nowhere else in life. Let us stay and listen.' Later, as we sat there, Vera turned to me and said, 'This is the first time I have ever seen these instruments being played.' I suddenly realised Vera was more than a coarse woman soldier, and denied access to the finer things of life.

As the afternoon drew to a close, Vera turned to me again and I noticed a sadness in her expression. 'It's time for me to leave,' she said. 'There is just time for me to catch the shuttle back for dinner tonight.'

'You don't need to go,' I said. 'Have dinner here with me at the hotel, and I'll walk you back to a later shuttle.'

She gave me a shy look, and nodded.

By this time dinner was being served in the dining room, and once again it was a moving experience for Vera who was unaccustomed to the waiters and fancy furniture. We chose a table near the wall, but even so, remained an unusual pair. Vera was the only woman in the room, as all the New Zealand nurses and WAACs had taken the opportunity to fly to Britain for ten days. Then to add to Vera's embarrassment, a violinist came across to our table and played several popular love songs to us, as only a violin can do! At last he left us to get on with the meal. It was ordinary army tucker, but when served on beautifully decorated china plates it was more like a royal serving.

By this time darkness had fallen, and we strolled arm in arm out to the terrace. It was one of those beautiful evenings with warm, still air under a sky full of stars. The night was an open invitation to romance.

'It is such a perfect night; would you like to come for a ride in a gondola?' I asked.

'I have seen them,' she said. 'But I've never thought of actually riding in one.'

'Here is your opportunity,' I said.

It took little to persuade her, and we were soon on our way. Together, we lay back in the gondola with Vera's head on my shoulder, and our arms around each other as we looked up into the starry, starry sky. From time to time our lips touched and moved sensually against each other. The only sound was an occasional snatch of music from the distant shore, and the gentle lapping of waves against the hull. In these idyllic surroundings I was reminded of an old song from the thirties:

> In my gondola, love, let us glide
> O'er the drowsy blue lagoon
> And float on the yellow tide
> Where sleeps a dreaming moon.

I quietly whispered the words to Vera, as they fitted

the scene and my mood perfectly, and perhaps that of Vera.

As we approached the other side of the lagoon we decided to go ashore at the Lido, a place where the wealthy of Venice had their homes and perfumed gardens. Arm in arm we strolled the quiet streets, stopping when the coast was clear for a hug and prolonged kiss before returning to the gondola. The return trip was pure romance. Anything further would have broken the romantic spell. As we approached the shore we each knew our magical night of romance was drawing to a close.

We stepped ashore and into a lighted area. Vera seemed a changed person. She walked with a jaunty air, as if her spirits had lifted, and her face seemed to glow with a new charm. She said nothing. Then her arm came around my back and she gave me a firm hug. As reality came back she stopped and turned to me. In a quiet voice she said, 'Our beautiful evening is coming to an end. There is just time for me to walk to the shuttle.' On the way we said little. In twofold silence we walked arm in arm, stopping on several occasions for a prolonged kiss.

I always remember her last words. 'If we never meet again I must tell you, you have introduced me to a beautiful way of life I never knew existed. Once I am out of the army I will never again accept the grime and suffering of the past. You have changed my life for ever.'

I watched her climb into the shuttle and disappear into its gloomy interior. Within minutes it drove away, leaving me wondering if it had all been a dream.

It was a rather pensive walk back to the hotel, as it is not every day that we change someone's life for ever. And naturally, I also considered it a very pleasant introduction to my holiday in Venice.

Six weeks later I was transferred to Florence to join the army of invasion of Japan.

My first day sightseeing there found me at the NAAFI for a cup of tea before returning to camp. As I sat contemplating my day at the Uffizi Gallery, I noticed a counter across the room selling cakes, and manned by the blonde I had talked with in Venice. I strolled across and said, 'Hello.'

She burst into a broad smile of recognition before saying, 'Well, don't just stand there. Come in and talk to me.' As she spoke she lifted the end of the counter to let me in.

'What on earth did you do to Vera?' she asked. 'Ever since her night out in Venice she has been walking on air. She had always been a bit sad and grumpy, but now she goes about singing and often laughs.' The blonde paused to let the significance of her words sink in. Then she said, 'Vera is a changed person. Two days ago she got secretly engaged to one of the NAAFI blokes.

This is against regulations, so don't mention it to anybody.' Once again she paused for a moment. 'As a matter of fact, she is out at the back now, washing dishes. Would you like to see her?'

'I'd be delighted,' I said.

She took my arm, and led me to the kitchen. There was Vera, up to her elbows in soapsuds. When she saw me she exclaimed, 'Hang on while I dry my hands.' Then she ran across to hug and kiss me.

With her arms still around me I said, 'I have just heard the good news, and I've come to wish you the best of good fortune for the years to come.' At that moment an officer appeared in the doorway. The blonde said, 'We'd better go now.' She took my arm again and quickly led me back to the dining room. I never saw Vera again.

It all happened many years ago, and I do hope she embraced her good fortune wisely. I regret never warning her of the pinion hidden in Fortuna's wing. It sometimes poisons good fortune.

Douglas Coop is a retired doctor who has worked in several countries and had dealings with peoples of diverse nationalities. As a senior medical consultant, he understands the emotions and differing points of view of people, and this shows in the varying characters and locations of his stories. He has written several other books.

For more details visit www.douglascoop.co.nz

The Price of Freedom

Crowds and Leadership

The Art of Influencing Crowds

Gone Missing

From the Sidelines of Music

That's Life

Seven Seasons of Wrath

Things My Father Never Told Me